The nuzzling felt quite pleasant. Very pleasant. Teresa did some nuzzling of her own.

"I have a room," Dawn whispered.

Magic words, Teresa thought. "I think I'm just about done with dancing for the night."

"At least standing up."

Dawn was a good kisser. Just the right amount of pressure followed by a nip on Teresa's lower lip. Teresa responded with a hungry nibble. It felt wonderful when Dawn's arms slid around her waist.

They weren't alone in the elevator, but all the twosomes seemed to have the same agenda they did.

Inside, it was a matter of moments before Teresa had Dawn's blouse unbuttoned.

A woman . . . Teresa felt like melting. The richness of skin, the texture of nipples—there was nothing that could compare to the feel of a woman's body against her own . . . Every nerve felt alive and aware that she was breast to breast with a soft and strong woman, k.d.'s crooning in the background.

LOOKING FOR NAIAD?

Buy our books at
www.naiadpress.com

or call our toll-free number
1-800-533-1973

or by fax (24 hours a day)
1-850-539-9731

Watermark

KARIN KALLMAKER

THE NAIAD PRESS, INC.
1999

Printed in the United States of America on acid-free paper
First Edition

Editor: Christine Cassidy
Cover designer: Bonnie Liss (Phoenix Graphics)
Typesetter: Sandi Stancil

Library of Congress Cataloging-in-Publication Data

Kallmaker, Karin, 1960 –
    Watermark / by Karin Kallmaker.
        p.   cm.
    ISBN 1-56280-235-6   (alk. paper)
    I. Title.
PS3561.A41665W38   1999
813'.54—dc21

98-46297
CIP

For Maria, still

The Ninth is for Never Never Land

About the Author

Karin Kallmaker was born in 1960 and raised by her loving, middle-class parents in California's Central Valley. The physician's Statement of Live Birth plainly declares: "Sex: Female" and "Cry: Lusty." Both are still true.

From a normal childhood and equally unremarkable public school adolescence, she went on to obtain an ordinary Bachelor's degree from the California State University at Sacramento. At the age of 16, eyes wide open, she fell into the arms of her first and only sweetheart. Ten years later, after seeing the film *Desert Hearts,* her sweetheart descended on the Berkeley Public Library determined to find some of "those" books. "Rule, Jane" led to "Lesbianism — Fiction" and then on to book after self-affirming book by and about lesbians. These books were the encouragement Karin needed to forget the so-called "mainstream" and spin her first romance for lesbians. That manuscript became her first Naiad Press novel, *In Every Port.* She now lives in the San Francisco Bay Area with that very same sweetheart; she is a one-woman woman. The happily-ever-after couple became Mom and Moogie to Kelson James in 1995 and Eleanor Delenn in 1997. They celebrated their twenty-first anniversary in 1998.

Also by Karin Kallmaker

Making Up for Lost Time

Embrace in Motion

Wild Things

Painted Moon

Car Pool

Paperback Romance

Touchwood

In Every Port

forthcoming: *Unforgettable*

Writing as Laura Adams

Night Vision

Christabel

forthcoming: *The Dawning*

1

"I can do this," Teresa repeated to herself. "I can do this." She squared her shoulders, certain the secretary was watching her, and went into the creative director's office.

She'd seen pictures of Rayann Germaine in the trades, and she'd been warned that "presence" was an understatement. Nevertheless, she was unprepared for the lurch in her stomach when two piercing brown eyes dissected her with a dispassionate flick. More than handsome, this woman exuded purpose. She reminded Teresa of the Renaissance portraits of Italian matriarchs — iron under silk. The array of awards neatly arranged on the shelf behind the desk heaped fuel onto Teresa's bonfire of insecurities.

She hoped it was a smile on her face as she crossed the room and sat down, relieved to find the chair wasn't one of those head game short ones that made her feel like a dwarf. Her relief was momentary. When she looked over the woman's shoulder the light glinted on a Clio award. Advertising's highest achievement, apart from money, was staring her right in the face.

Her rehearsed greeting faltered in her throat. Ten seconds and her first meeting with the director was not going as she had planned.

"You have the storyboards, right?" Ms. Germaine gestured for the boards with the air of someone whose time was extremely limited. While it was probably true, it made Teresa feel like a delivery clerk.

Teresa handed them over. She was really proud of the way they had turned out, especially after having had to learn an unfamiliar system in the past two days. Between the time that she had accepted the job and her first day they had changed over their software to a package she wasn't nearly so expert with. Her supervisor had said she'd catch on and she had. This was her first opportunity to show her results to the —

"This is not what the client wants."

Teresa fought the urge to gulp. "I talked to them this morning. They've changed their mind seven times in the past two days, but this is their current concept. Mom in a *white* car, mom in kitchen, not baby's room, product break, fade."

"Did you talk to Artie?"

Teresa shook her head. She was too much of a plebe to talk to Artie.

The director seemed at the edge of her patience. "Artie wants car, product break, baby's room, fade. As per two hours ago."

"No one told me," Teresa said. She wished the woman would at least look at her.

"Just do them over. Call Artie's office and let them know they're on the way."

"Did he say how he wants to transition —" The phone buzzed and Teresa swallowed the last of her sentence.

"When? No, that's not what she wants. Listen to me. *Listen* to me. Do I have your attention? That's not what she wants. How many times do I have to explain it? You don't want me to stop by again, believe me."

Geez, this woman was on some sort of power trip. Okay, so she was the head of the creative department at Hand & Hoke, one of the west coast's most *outré* ad agencies. So she'd crafted the campaigns that made household names of new companies. So she'd won awards and made a lot of people a lot of money. But who would have thought she'd talk to someone on the phone like that? She was acting like some diva when she wasn't ten years older than Teresa, even though the brown hair was flecked with gray. So beautifully flecked, in fact, that it couldn't be natural, Teresa decided. Meow.

"I am *not* balking at the money. It doesn't matter. Nothing matters except that everything be the way she wants it. And she wants the minimum, the bare minimum, and I want to be able to tell her truthfully that that is exactly what she's going to get. If that is pine, then that's — What? I don't want to see it again. Look, you're supposed to be providing the service here. Everything was already supposed to be settled when we bought the package and now you want more decisions. Christ. Okay. Someone — not me — will be by soon."

Teresa knew not to say a word while the woman dialed another number. She'd seen her grandmother in too many towering rages to mistake one when she saw it. She'd been told this woman was *nice*, for Christ's sake, one of the most influential people in advertising in the city and a lesbian, too. She had jumped at this job for exactly those reasons, even though it meant several years of menial graphic design. She'd been certain she'd learn a lot.

"Danny? Those assholes won't finish unless someone actually sees the thing and approves it. I can't go there again."

Then she glanced at Teresa. Teresa didn't think she'd ever forget it. She glanced, then closed her eyes and said bitterly, "She's got me in exile. I'm surrounded by bumbling amateurs and I just can't take it."

Teresa sat there blinking, wondering if that remark had been directed at her. Of course it had. Amateur? *Amateur?* A Master's in Fine Arts and this woman called her an amateur?

She had to be on the edge of a breakdown, Teresa decided. Rage was gone; now the manicured hand wrapped around the phone was white-knuckled. The other trembled on the desk. She was listening intently and Teresa knew her presence had been forgotten.

"Thank you," she said, almost in a whisper. "I don't know what I'd do without you."

Teresa couldn't decide how to break the silence after the phone call ended. A cough was contrived. Perhaps she should just begin speaking? No, the time for that had slipped away. She shifted her weight and the chair creaked faintly.

The director jumped. "Weren't we done?"

"Um, no, not quite. Did Artie say how he wanted the transition from break to home?"

"No, he didn't. This is one of our biggest clients. Think of something . . . creative. This is the creative department. That's what we do here."

Teresa skulked back to her workstation. It was an hour before she stopped shaking sufficiently to handle more than just rearranging the art order for printing. She gulped down a huge cup of coffee while she worked. It didn't help the trembling but it made her brain start functioning again. She decided to transition from the product description by zooming in through the product logo to the setting of the mother tidying up in the baby's room. The deep green of the logo, recently freshened up by the folks across the hall in the sigils and icons department, could be carried over to anything in the baby's room for visual continuity.

She left a message for the client saying the story-boards would be over right away. But she couldn't send them without the director's final okay. Her boss, Sandra, had been very clear about that.

Even though the secretary said it was okay to go in, she knocked and stuck her head in as if the door were a shield. Rayann was on the phone but waved her forward.

She turned over the boards without stopping her conversation, nodding absently. When she got to the transition shot she frowned, said, "Hold on" into the receiver and covered it with her hand. To Teresa, she snapped, "We can't send them something like this. Do it over. This client is a traditionalist. If you can't think of anything else, use a fade to gray — side wash maybe. Indicate it as less than two seconds." She glanced at Teresa, then back at the boards. "This is too art school."

Teresa blinked at her, then her mouth took over. "I guess you're right." Her voice shook a little too much to be scathing, but she tried. "I'm just a summa cum laude M.F.A. with a piddly year's study at the Sorbonne, and I'm sure that's influencing my work."

The director said into the phone, "Hold on one more minute." Then she fixed Teresa with her cold, piercing gaze. "You want to be an artist, go be an artist. Been there, done that. But the truth is I'm here because I *like* advertising. That's why you need to be here. Georgia O'Keeffe is my favorite artist, but I wouldn't want her doing storyboards for baby food." Back to the phone she went. "I'm here."

Teresa made it to the bathroom before she dissolved into tears. Too art school? Just who did that — that bitch think she was? She had treated Teresa like a robot without any feelings or ego or experience or *anything*. She must have an incredible PR machine to have convinced the advertising community she was not only talented but *nice*. Teresa usually regretted moments when her mouth took over her good sense, and lord knows she'd had plenty of practice removing her size sevens from her mouth, but this time she was glad.

Hoping none of her coworkers would notice her red-rimmed eyes, Teresa finished the fade-to-gray storyboard and gave the bundle to the receptionist for messenger service.

She sat at her workstation and muttered, "I gave up an assistant curator's position — a job actually relevant to my Master of Fine Arts degree — to be treated like dirt by some power dyke on steroids." Christ, it looked like her father was right. His no-strings advice had been to forget the money difference, take the job her heart would be happy to go to every day. She'd told him she was going to have to start making her own decisions sometime. Ever so gently, he'd pointed out that independence did not mean she couldn't agree with him. He had been right, she decided. Business sucked.

Sandra hurried into her cubicle with a breezy, "Knock, knock." She continued in her usual breathy way, "The boards are on the way, right? I really have to apologize for giving you something so important. You just haven't been here long enough to know all the ins and outs of the client."

"Did she complain?"

Sandra seemed to understand who "she" was. "No, she just reminded me that our biggest clients should get our more experienced people. And she's been under a lot of personal stress lately. But don't worry, you'll catch on."

Teresa was sure that Miz High-and-Mighty Germaine had chewed Sandra out for letting the bumbling art-school amateur work on something "so important." Hell, it was just the storyboards for a 15-second spot. Personal stress was no excuse for treating people badly, including that poor person on the phone.

When she got up the next morning, Teresa called Carla Hascom and asked point-blank if the museum job was still available. It wasn't. She dragged herself to work, dreading anything that might cause her path to cross with the creative director's. The woman had made her feel like a bug. No, less than that — like bug poop.

The day was hectic and not as bad as the previous one, but she couldn't keep her job blues out of her voice when her father called that night.

"I know something's wrong, punkin. Tell your old man all about it."

"Oh, Daddy. You're going to say 'I told you so.' "

"I wouldn't —"

"You do it all the time."

"I was going to say, if you'll let me finish . . ." Her father knew how to pause for effect.

Teresa sighed. "Please continue, Mr. Alan Mandrell, sir, maestro. I await the pearls of your wisdom."

He snorted. "I wouldn't say I told you so until after we'd come up with a solution to whatever your problem is. Then I'd say it."

Teresa's chuckle got lost in the T-shirt she pulled over her head. She cradled the phone into her shoulder as she pulled her shoulder-length hair into a ponytail. "Well, I hate my job. Not even a week and I hate it. The creative director is a bitch."

"And she was the reason you took the job. I'd say that's a problem. Of course, you can't always work with people you like."

"She called me a — a bumbling amateur."

"The woman is a Philistine, obviously. The Queen

of Mean. So what are you going to do?" His unconditional support was soothing.

"Stick it out for a while, I guess." She made a scrunchy face in the mirror. Was that a wrinkle? She peered closer.

"Well, keep your eye on the paper, and put the word out. You never know when something might come along. And whatever you do, don't let your mouth get you into trouble."

"Me? I have my verbal impulses fully under control, thank you." It *was* a wrinkle. Radiating outward from the corner of her left eye. Crap.

"Did you check back at the museum? Reese?"

"Ya? Oh, well, I guess I'll do that. I have a wrinkle! Work is aging me already."

Her father did not need to laugh quite so hard. "Honey, think of them as character lines. It shows you have some."

"Puh-lease. Men have character lines."

"*Au contraire*, punkin." Her father was warming to his theme. "You can either look like Isabella Rossellini or Cher. I'll take Isabella any day. Don't get me wrong. I have no problems with Cher's character, but she's starting to look a little . . . preserved."

"Her mother probably didn't look like Ingrid Bergman as a starting place."

"Yours did." She could hear the smile and hint of wistfulness in his voice.

"Oh, Daddy. You are too sweet to be a man." She stretched the skin over her left temple. The wrinkle was still there. How long had this been going on?

"Don't be sexist. I raised you better than that."

9

"How's Melanie?" She pressed down hard on her nose, which in her opinion was a little too pointy.

The red herring worked. Her father said, with great enthusiasm, "She is just wonderful. In fact, that's why I called."

Teresa felt a chill of warning — she had had a feeling about Melanie. Daddy had been seeing her for over a year. "Why?"

"Mel and I are going to get married."

"Wow. Congratulations." She said it with all her heart. She meant it, really she did. But it would take some getting used to. It had been just the two of them for as long as she could remember. "When?"

"Vegas isn't even an hour's flight from L.A. so we thought we'd do it there — a couple of months from now. Mel can't really take any vacation until the real estate market cools off in the late fall, and we don't want to wait that long."

"What's the rush? You haven't done anything you're not supposed to, have you?" Teresa smirked at her reflection. He'd walked right into that one.

Her father was not perturbed. "Yes, we have. But we were as safe as I expect you to be."

"Oh, man. An admission of fooling around combined with a parental lecture. You're sharp, today, Dad."

"Just practicing until you give me grandchildren." His gale of laughter made the line crackle.

"Daddy!" She felt fifteen again, when she'd informed him that she had no maternal instincts. "There's very little hope of that."

He sobered, but only slightly, and said, "I'm aware of that, but a father can dream."

"I don't know what Melanie sees in you," she teased.

"Me, neither. Don't tell her, okay? Anyway, is there a chance you could get away long enough to fly to Vegas? Our treat, of course. Melanie really wants you there. Her son — you have to meet Ken sometime — is going to make it, too."

"Wild horses and bitchy creative directors can't keep me away."

They chatted a while longer and Teresa sat there for a few minutes with her hand on the receiver. Married! He hadn't exactly been a monk while she'd been growing up, but as far as she knew, he'd never been serious about anyone after her mother's death. That was — twenty-seven years. Wow.

She was startled by the phone chirping under her hand. Daddy probably forgot something.

"Hi, Teresa, this is Carla Hascom. Have I caught you at a bad time?"

"No," she said, surprised.

"The person we hired — really, our distant second choice — just called me and said she's not going to show up tomorrow. She took another job. Do you believe that? She was supposed to start tomorrow. Are you still interested?"

"Very! I just have to give two weeks' notice. I don't want to burn my bridges too badly. This is so exciting." She bounced on her chair.

"I do want to ask why you're giving up the job you chose."

"I made a mistake," she said easily. "A cost of youth, maybe? I don't think I'm cut out for the business world. I miss school and thinking about art all day." And my talents are completely unappreciated, she added silently, especially by that vicious witch.

"Well, you won't think about it all day here." Teresa heard a smile in Carla's voice.

"I know. I'm in for a lot of database and scut work. I can deal."

"Great. I can't help but think everything worked out for the best."

"Me, too. So I'll see you in . . . two weeks from tomorrow? The eighteenth?"

"Sounds great. I am really enthused, and the board will be delighted."

Teresa did a little dance around the apartment and left a happy note for her roommate, Vivian. She'd whined Vivian's ear off last night. Then she slipped her favorite Madonna mix into the Walkman and set out for her run.

The steady *thup thup* of her Air Nikes on the pavement gave rise to a feel-good chant: *bye-bye, Queena Meana, bye-bye.*

She was just putting down her things the next morning when Sandra chivied her into a meeting with the director and a copywriter she knew by sight only. He was hard to miss — rainbow hair and multiple studs in each ear. She had wanted to give Sandra her notice right away, but she settled into her chair at the small conference table and realized it would have to wait for a more private moment.

"We've been invited to submit a concept to Prime Life Beverage Company," Rayann was saying.

Teresa said nothing as Sandra and the copywriter

jabbered about the possibility of getting the business. She felt liberated, knowing she wouldn't have to work on it.

"Prime Life's new C.E.O. *says* he wants to freshen up their image, do something avant-garde —"

The copywriter guffawed. "What, we're going to use all caps in the copy? That'll make the front page of *Advertising Age*."

Sandra said to Teresa, "All clients say they want avant-garde. All they mean is something slightly different."

Rayann went briskly on, "Yes, if we all had a dollar for every time a client said 'different — but not *that* different' — we'd be rich. We have about two weeks to do the proposal and have something to show them that proves that we alone understand their business and have the resources to care for their business the way it deserves to be cared for."

Teresa thought Rayann was the most cynical person she'd ever met. It was hard to believe she personally did pro bono work for about two dozen women's and gay charities. Some of the commercials had brought tears to Teresa's eyes. She had thought the brain behind them was reaching out with genuine human caring and warmth. But all Rayann Germaine was good at was manipulating emotions.

"It's their coffee market they're really looking to boost, and coffee ads are at least by and large aimed at the literate."

Sandra put her hand over her heart in a mock faint. "Dare I dream? Classical music?"

Rayann made a face. "The C.E.O. apparently likes Yanni."

The copywriter screamed while Sandra swooned.

"Enough, enough," Rayann said. She shoved several thick folders at Sandra. "Here's the background info they gave me and some I picked up myself. Do a Nexus on the decision makers and pull in anyone else you need."

Her gaze flicked to Teresa as she said it and Teresa couldn't help herself. "You might need someone to balance out my limited art-school repertoire." She might have gotten away with it if she'd laughed or at least smiled. But she didn't.

Rayann Germaine blinked, as if she wasn't sure what she had heard or couldn't recall why it was being said. Then she shrugged. It clearly was not important to her. She turned pointedly to Sandra. "I won't be around much to supervise this, so I'd appreciate it if you're careful."

"I understand," Sandra said. She was actually favoring Rayann with a gentle smile. "Don't worry about it. I'll take care of it."

Teresa wondered what kind of magic spell the witch Rayann had on Sandra. The knowledge that she had another job took all the restraints off her tongue. She said in a little-girl voice, "And I'll try weawy weawy hard to be creative, because I've been told that's what we do here." As soon as the words were out of her mouth she regretted them. Her stupid mouth. She felt herself reddening.

Sandra was looking at her with disapproval while the copywriter just stared.

Rayann Germaine blinked again, as if she had finally realized where she'd met Teresa before. "Is this about the other day? This is the advertising business. If you are easily offended and can't get over it in less than fifteen minutes you'll get an ulcer by the end of the month. We don't have time to sulk, and right now I don't need attitude." She glanced at her watch. "And I'm late for an appointment."

"You won't have to put up with my attitude, since I quit."

Sandra gawked. "Teresa, what are you talking about?"

So much for not burning bridges, but she couldn't stop now. "Nothing against you, Sandra. I just want to work somewhere that treats me like a human being and gives just a little bit of respect."

"Respect is earned," Rayann snapped. She said in a flat voice, "Fine. Best of luck. Sayonara. I just do not have time. Sandra, get Juana on this instead."

"She'll be perfect," Sandra said, after a gulp.

Teresa found herself in the hallway with Sandra, who looked both angry and incredulous.

"You were serious, weren't you? Well, it doesn't matter, it's a done deal."

"I — I don't know what to say." She couldn't begin to explain what had spurred her behavior. Her stupid mouth had independent wiring sometimes. She swallowed hard and vowed it would be the last time.

"Never mind," Sandra said. "This was obviously not the right fit. You can tidy up your desk and we'll call it quits."

"I was planning to work out two weeks' notice," Teresa stammered.

"It won't be necessary, under the circumstances. I'm sorry this didn't work out." Sandra stalked away.

Teresa sat down in a daze. She hadn't really made any new acquaintances — there was no one she felt obligated to say good-bye to. It would be as if she'd never been here, which felt strange. But wasn't that what she wanted?

Well, she certainly hadn't wanted to lose two weeks' pay. Making the next rent was going to be tough, and all because of her lack of control. All because some other lesbian had treated her badly. The Queen of Mean was an understatement — and cheating her out of two weeks' pay!

She gathered up her few belongings and stormed out of the building, working herself up to raw fury. That she might have been even partially responsible for her predicament only made her more angry. She was most of the way home when she realized that Carla Hascom might be very glad to have Teresa start tomorrow — she'd make the rent after all.

But that did not make Rayann Germaine any less a bitch. And as far as the world of advertising was concerned — it was the Seventh Circle of Hell.

She was well out of it.

2

"Under the circumstances, you're doing a great job."

"It's not good enough," Rayann said. "And I have to be honest, Tony. I don't want to be here. I'm only here because I told her I would." Through the window behind him, she could see the shadows lengthening. Another day ending that she should have spent with Louisa.

Tony Hand pressed his lips together, seeming to choose his words carefully. "I understand, you know that."

"I know — Aaron made you go to work, too."

"And I did not want to be here. And all things considered, looking back, nothing truly lasting or good came of my being here instead of with him."

She had been holding on to the hope that it was for the best that she continue to work instead of spending all her time with Louisa. Tony was telling her it wasn't. She made the decision her heart was longing to make. "Memorial Day was like a gift — an extra day with her that I didn't have to come here. Holidays and weekends are not enough, no matter what she says. We don't have enough of them left. So I'm going to try to change her mind."

Tony nodded, then he took on more of his head honcho demeanor. "You know that time marches on in this place like nowhere else. There are at least seven people itching for your job."

"I know. I was hoping I could take a leave." Technically, it was her right to take up to four months' leave without jeopardizing her job.

"That's what I'll announce, that you're on indefinite leave." He sighed. "The lawyers tell me not to say things like this, Ray, but you know I can't guarantee that you'll be at the top of creative when you return."

"I know that. I accept it."

"I don't want to lose you, and I'll do my best when you're ready to come back."

"I know that, too." She blinked back tears, caught off guard by a rush of tenderness for Tony, all out of proportion to their working relationship and workplace friendship.

He cleared his throat. "Go get Lou to agree."

The drive to the hospital was so well known by

now that she didn't take note of anything along the journey from the financial district of San Francisco to Oakland's pill hill. There were the usual stalled cars blocking lanes and trucks driving way over the speed limit. Just like every weeknight for the last eight weeks, the end of her journey from work was not home, but Louisa's hospital room.

How could it be almost two months since she had put down the phone in her office, not believing what she had just been told? It was a hoax, she had thought. A policeman with a sick sense of humor.

Her first thought was to call Teddy, Louisa's son. He was probably at the courthouse, he could get to the bottom of this . . . this impossibility.

She gave a garbled account of the phone call to Teddy's assistant, who said, "Oh my God," and hung up after promising to get Teddy as soon as possible.

In a minute, maybe two, her private line rang.

"Ray, what's going on?" Teddy's voice was abnormally high.

"I think it was some kind of joke. A police officer, someone who said he was from Oakland P.D., said your mom was hit by a truck. That's nonsense. She was only going over to the lake. It has to be a joke. It's someone else."

"Did you call the bookstore?"

Of course. What a simple solution. "I'll do it right now."

"Keep me on the line."

As the speed dial pulsed she could hear Teddy very faintly repeating, "Oh my God, oh my God."

The bookstore line rang until the voice mail picked up. "Lou, I need you to call me. Right away. Let me know you're okay. Call me, it's important."

19

"There's no answer," she reported to Teddy.

"What hospital did they take her to?"

"Bay Summit, but it's not her."

"Ray —"

"It can't be her!"

"I'm at the courthouse, and I've got my car. I can be downstairs in fifteen minutes. We'll go together. Stay there. I'll be there as soon as I can. Okay?"

"Okay." She looked around her office in a fog. It was so silly. She didn't have time for this.

None of it was happening. But if it would make Teddy feel better, she'd go with him to the hospital. But by the time they got there, she was certain Louisa would be back at the bookstore.

"Cancel my appointments for the day," she told her secretary as she left.

Fiona's eyebrows disappeared under her bangs. "What should I tell people?"

"Something personal came up," Rayann said over her shoulder. "Someone thinks Lou was in some sort of accident, but it's all a mistake I've got to straighten out."

"You're kidding!"

"No lie." She held the elevator door open for one more second. "And give anything urgent to Sandra."

As she stood on the curb awaiting Teddy, she had noticed the sharp smell of pretzels and hot dogs, the creak of an armored car, the cloud of exhaust from a cab. Some tourist was navigating a motorhome down Montgomery Street when noon hour was approaching. The map on the side of the motorhome showed they hadn't yet been to Nebraska. She had noticed it all, would remember it all. None of it had seemed real.

* * * * *

She realized abruptly she was parked in the garage across the street from the hospital and that it had been a while since she'd turned off the engine. There was only an hour left until the nurses would kick her out.

Her original impressions of the heartlessness of medical personnel were long gone. Even the doctors had redeemed themselves, showing caring and affection. They'd been gentle and kind and willing to talk with Louisa even though her responses took so long.

She stopped at the nurse's station to check on Louisa's day and found that nothing had changed. Once she had regained consciousness after the accident, Louisa had shown no signs of the steady loss of liver and kidney function the doctors had told them to expect. She was caught between better and worse.

The beeps, hisses and hums of all the equipment in the room faded away, as they always did when Rayann leaned down so she could talk quietly into Louisa's ear. They had so often talked seriously while tangled in sheets and each other. Recapturing their intimacy, if only for a moment, was like snatching heaven to Rayann.

"I know you want me to keep on with my life, but leaving you every day is killing me." Rayann had never been able to hide tears, and the mixture of pain and compassion in Louisa's eyes did not help. "I know you don't want me to lose my job. I know you don't want anyone waiting on you. I know you don't want to be a burden, but I can't concentrate, I'm forgetting things, I snap at everybody. My being there makes

21

people think I'm actually checking their work. Please let me stay with you." She rubbed the ring Louisa had given her eight years ago. "That's what this was supposed to mean."

Louisa closed her eyes. She carefully moved her right hand to the language card that helped her communicate when she was too tired to talk. Rayann could only guess the fury of helplessness that Louisa felt, reduced to pointing at the word *yes* on a card because a bastard drunk driver ran a red light.

"Thank you." Rayann heard Danny come in and she turned, not bothering to hide the tears that Danny had seen too many times in the last two months. Louisa's best friend had become Rayann's steady rock. "I'm not in exile anymore."

Danny immediately understood. "Lou, you did the right thing. It was killing her." Rayann marveled how Danny could talk and act like nothing had changed. Rayann had discovered a deep core of serenity under the steel gray cap of hair and bomber jacket.

"Listen, Lou. Ray asked me to check out the funeral home and what they're doing. They tried to talk me into some water-sealed, lead-lined cherry wood job that cost about as much as a Space Shuttle. I practically had to call the Better Business Bureau to get them to admit that you and Ray had prepaid all this stuff with them and that there was no reason why you had to pick again. But now they remember."

Rayann was so happy Danny had gone instead of her. She would have just cried and yelled and cried some more — her entire repertory of emotions these last two months.

"Then," Danny continued, "get this. They want to know when you're going to need it." She rubbed her short gray hair. "I told them, look, she's pretty sick right now and we just want to put her mind at ease on this. She'll probably outlive all of us. I am not making an appointment here."

Rayann gulped and turned to fiddle with the flowers Teddy had brought yesterday. She had not realized until now that Danny still had hope. Suddenly she knew she didn't have any more hope and the wave of guilt threatened to buckle her knees.

A nurse came in to check Louisa's vitals and adjust the morphine drip for the night dosage. Louisa fell asleep soon after, the deeply etched lines of pain somewhat relaxed. Danny went home to Marilyn while Rayann made her end-of-the-night phone call to Teddy.

She had no reason to stay. She had no reason to leave, either. Every night she went home to their empty house. When they'd moved in on Valentine's day they had been full of plans, but the renovations were only half-complete. Faucets dripped, wallpaper sat gathering dust. The impatiens and marigolds they'd planted in the backyard the weekend before the accident withered for lack of water. She could afford to pay someone to finish what she and Louisa had been doing on weekends, but that would take planning ahead and thinking about the future.

The future didn't bear thinking about. The present was nearly intolerable. She could hardly deal with the past. The past didn't even seem real.

The nurses had first assumed she was Teddy's wife. The doctor who explained how serious the internal injuries and broken bones were talked mostly to Teddy, who took it all in with ragged composure. He had clutched her as if she was his life preserver, while she continued to believe with all her heart that it was one colossal mistake.

Only when they had finally been allowed to see Louisa — Teddy overrode the doctor's suggestion that only he should go in — did she admit there was no mistake.

Louisa's luxurious black and silver hair was matted with sweat, her soft skin translucent and clammy. Her right arm and leg were in plaster and traction. The tender, expressive mouth was hidden behind a respirator and masses of tape.

Rayann could only gasp to Teddy, "It's not her, it's not her," while he cradled her against him, hiding his tears in her hair.

"She may regain consciousness once the shock subsides, but that could be too much to hope for. Do you know what her wishes are?" The doctor was talking to Teddy again.

Rayann could not let go of Teddy. She had the papers at home, but couldn't consider leaving to get them. She said, "Do whatever it takes. The insurance is good — I have money."

The doctor was shaking his head slightly at Teddy. Later, Rayann realized that the doctor was assuming Teddy would be strong and rational, be a man.

To Rayann, he said, "It's not a matter of money. She was gravely injured. According to the police, the truck was going approximately thirty-five miles an hour and she was thrown twenty-two feet." He looked at Teddy again. "I need to know what her wishes are."

"Rayann has her power of attorney."

"That's you?"

She nodded miserably. "It's at home."

The doctor was clearly confused. "What is your relationship to the patient?" He looked down at his chart.

"I'm her partner. Her lover."

The doctor looked as nonplussed as most people did. "And you have her power of attorney for health care decisions?"

"Yes, it's at home." After an acquaintance had been ousted from her partner's hospital room by hostile family, they had taken the time to get all their paperwork in order — wills, powers of attorney and joint ownership of the bookstore and the new house.

The doctor looked at Teddy, who suddenly stiffened. "I am her only child and I'm telling you that Ms. Germaine is my mother's partner and will make all the decisions regarding her care. I don't want there to be any confusion about that."

"There won't be," the doctor said. "I'm putting it in the chart. But we'll need the document when it's convenient. Soon." He looked at Rayann. "And what are her wishes?"

"Do whatever it takes," Rayann repeated. Why were they arguing about it?

"Ray," Teddy said softly, "what if they can't do anything more?"

She could picture in her mind the X in the box

next to "Do Not Resuscitate." Lou had been very clear about it. No machines, no heroic efforts, no living as a vegetable. If she couldn't communicate she didn't want to live. Rayann gulped. Louisa's fingers moved slowly, as if she dreamed.

"Do whatever it takes," she repeated. "Would you even be asking if she were twenty?"

"Yes, I would have to ask."

Teddy said softly, "Mom and I talked about what she wanted. Do you want me to tell him?"

She turned her face away from Teddy's gentleness. Though it had taken her a while to uncover it, he had the same wealth of sensitivity that his mother did. "No," she whispered.

"Is it DNR?" The doctor had his pen poised.

"Ray?"

She could not say it. She felt him nodding and the pain in her chest was so severe she could not breathe. She heard the doctor's pen on the chart. DNR. Do Not Resuscitate.

"When will she wake up?" she heard Teddy ask.

"If she regains consciousness, it won't be in less than three hours — probably six. If she doesn't within twelve, then she probably won't."

Rayann found the doctor's dispassionate tones absolutely loathsome. The man was a monster.

"She's very strong," Teddy said.

"As I suspected." The doctor slung his stethoscope around his neck. "She wouldn't have survived the surgery if she wasn't. We did what we could. There was a lot of shattered bone, and four major organs were damaged. We don't know yet if any will regain even partial function."

"Is there —" Teddy's voice broke. He coughed. "Is there any chance?"

Rayann looked up, watching every expression on the doctor's face.

"Where there is life, there is hope," the doctor said quietly. "But if this were my loved one I'd make the very, very most of the times she is conscious. If she is conscious," he said more briskly, "I or someone else will explain the situation to her. And if she wants to change her instructions she can, of course."

"I doubt she will," Teddy said. "She has strong feelings about it."

The doctor nodded and left.

Teddy helped her sit down in the only chair. "I'm going to make some phone calls. Will you be okay?"

"No." Her voice shook.

"I know." He left so quickly she knew he was hiding his tears again.

Time was only broken by the clicking of the automatic drip and the grind of the blood pressure machine.

The next thing Rayann was consciously aware of was a raised voice outside the room.

"I'm sorry, it's the rules."

"My best friend is in there and I'm going to see her."

"The family has to consent."

Rayann opened the door with relief. "Danny, please, come in."

The nurse said sharply, "Is this okay with her son?"

Rayann replied, equally sharply, "I say who visits her, and yes, it is okay with him."

Danny looked tiny in her bomber jacket, all the swagger of her usual step gone. "Oh, Lou," she whispered, as she caressed the back of Louisa's hand. "Oh, Lou."

Teddy slipped in after a few minutes. Part of Rayann took note of him holding Danny's hand as they stood next to Louisa's bed. That alone was a remarkable thing. Ten years ago Rayann had been running away from a bad love affair when Louisa had offered to rent her the other bedroom in the apartment over the bookstore that Louisa owned. At that time Teddy wouldn't stay in the same room with the obviously butch Danny because of what Danny's overt lesbianism meant about his mother — that his mother was a lesbian, too. Louisa's love for Rayann had been one of the reasons his attitudes had changed.

A long time later, Teddy's wife, Joyce, arrived with Tucker. He came to Rayann's side, white-faced but composed.

"Is Grandma going to wake up?" In typical teenaged fashion, his fists were jammed into the pockets of his Forty-Niners jacket that was too big at the waist and too small at the shoulders. He shook his hair out of his eyes the same way he always did when his grandmother asked him to.

"Maybe," Rayann managed. Her voice was raspy and she realized she was very thirsty. "I hope so."

"Okay." He brightened and Rayann realized he'd thought if Louisa woke up she would get better. Later, she would ask herself if that was the moment she had given up hope.

For the hundredth time she told herself that it wasn't happening.

Joyce pressed one hand sympathetically to Rayann's shoulder. Rayann had liked Joyce the moment she had entered Teddy's life four years ago. She was very good with Tucker without trying to alter the already secure relationship between father and son. "If there's anything, Ray. You know that."

Rayann nodded.

Joyce said to Tucker, "It's time to go talk to your father about Grandma Lou."

He nodded, gave Rayann the half hug his fifteen-year old dignity could manage, and then said to Louisa, "Get better, Grandma."

Louisa's eyelids fluttered and Rayann's heart felt as if it would burst. "She hears you, Tuck."

Louisa's eyes opened. She blinked slowly, then tried to turn her head. After a few moments several of the machines began beeping excitedly and the officious nurse burst in.

"Everyone must go. The doctor will be here right away."

Joyce took Tucker out, telling him they would come back soon.

Rayann leaned over Louisa. "I'm here, I'm here."

Louisa's dark brown eyes were filled with apprehension and pain.

"Don't try to talk, just rest. The doctor is coming. I'm here, Teddy is here. Danny will be back in a little bit. Don't worry."

Louisa closed her eyes after trying to nod.

"Ms. Germaine, you really must leave." It was not the same doctor who had first met them and Rayann wondered if he'd even read Louisa's chart.

"Why?"

"Because I need to do an exam and have a very specific conversation with the patient. Another presence can make that hard."

"If I was legally her wife would you make me leave?"

The doctor took a deep breath. "I know this is difficult, and yes, I would."

She had leaned against the wall outside the room, eyes closed. She hadn't even felt as if she was on the planet, let alone in a hospital. Anger, frustration, grief and disbelief had swirled inside her but she had told herself she needed to be in control, for Louisa's sake.

Control, that was a laugh. Rayann turned out all the lights in the house as if that would hide the tears. Tears and anger got the better of her every day. It was such a relief not to have to go to work. What a waste of time — picking out a suit, dithering over hose and shoes, trying to get yet another account, make yet another bonus. None of it meant a damn thing.

Even with that load eased from her mind, she wondered where she would find the endurance to get up and go on. She wanted no part of tomorrow.

3

What to wear to a board meeting? The question had been plaguing Teresa for the last three weeks. Her serious career wear was limited to her interview suit, which had suffered from an oil smear on a Muni train. Her other clothes were more appropriate for an ad agency. The D'Angelo Museum board was too conservative for sweaters and leggings.

Yesterday she'd bought a vintage suit at one of her favorite shops on Fillmore Street, but she was in serious need of new shoes. Her adored Doc Martens were right out, and her "dress" shoes were showing their age — they dated from before graduate school and they'd seen a lot of dances and interviews.

She pondered the pair of Aldos she really liked — black with their distinctive wide heel — but the price tag was still taking her breath away. They'd look smashing with the heavy raw silk that made up the suit. Think of it this way, she told herself. If you were still working at that ad agency you could afford a closet full of shoes. One good pair won't break the bank.

She took another turn around the store. It was making her salivate. There was a pair of simple not-too-high heels, black patent, that screamed "business-woman" and might make her seem a little more experienced — but hell. Did she really want to play that game?

You're only young once — why not look it? Because she was asking the board for an increase in their badly underestimated budget for modernizing the museum's collection database. She didn't want them to think she was some upstart brat who didn't know what she was talking about, three weeks on the job and full of ways to spend more money. Carla thought it very important that the board members get a chance to meet her and hear directly from her what she proposed to do.

So what's it gonna be, she asked herself. Fun or competence? And make up your mind before you're late back to work. It was less than a Muni stop back to Yerba Buena Gardens, but she'd already been gone forty minutes.

Unsure what to do, she let her credit card take

over and left the store with both pairs of shoes. She would try them on tonight and get her roommate's opinion. Vivian could be counted on to have definite feelings on any fashion subject. Now, that was a plan. Thank God it was settled. She didn't want to turn into the kind of person who obsessed about her appearance. She had three years until she turned thirty. She could obsess then.

She caught a glimpse of herself in the mirrors that lined the curved escalator. As usual she squinted at the wrinkle that refused to go away. Obsessed? Mildly, she thought. She'd switched from cheap shampoo because Vivian said it would eventually ruin her hair, and now she used only Cetaphil on her face — more of Vivian's advice on How to Stay Young. What was gentle enough for a baby's butt was gentle enough for her skin.

If she followed all of Vivian's advice, however, she'd give up running, which Vivian swore would make her bosoms sag. Vivian, who avoided vulgarity at all costs, had blanched when Teresa had said it was a poor choice to make — sagging tits or a fat ass.

She needed a moisturizer and Vivian had dictated a brand only available at a cosmetics counter in finer stores. She braved the perfume samplers at the Nordstrom entrance and lingered next to a cosmetics display offering a free bottle of cologne for a purchase over sixty dollars.

A clerk, clad in a white lab jacket and meticulously made up and coiffed, immediately offered her services. "Are you looking for something to protect your skin from airborne toxins? Or UV damage?"

"Well, I have this wrinkle." The darned thing was getting deeper no matter how much Cetaphil she rubbed into it.

"Well, we girls must expect such things when we're in our thirties."

Thirties? *Thirties?* How terrible did she look? She glanced in the mirror — she looked ghastly. Or was that just the lighting? "What do you recommend?"

"The most important thing is a good, gentle cleanser. Our cleanser can be used with or without water. Here —" she dribbled a dollop onto Teresa's fingertips. "Doesn't that feel smooth?"

She rubbed the solution around her fingertips. It felt and looked like Cetaphil to her.

"Used with our deep-cleansing pack, the pores on your face will start to breathe again. Do you use any makeup at all?"

"No, not really. Not enough time."

Another bottle appeared on the counter. "This is our premiere foundation. After the foundation comes our perfect match cover that will hide all those little imperfections."

"Is that what you use?"

"Oh, of course. Would you believe that I am forty-seven?"

Teresa looked at the woman carefully. Another bottle appeared on the counter, then a palette of eye shadows. Her mental cash register was ringing. No, she didn't believe this woman was forty-seven. "Actually, I just wanted a good moisturizer."

Two more bottles joined the growing pile on the counter. "Our patented astringent removes all the excess oils, then our moisturizer restores the natural moisture balance to your skin. In use with the cleanser and foundation you are virtually assured that your skin is clean, moist and smooth."

Smooth again. The word du jour.

"Shall I ring this up? Today is a good day to start working on your new, younger look."

She guessed the total was well over two hundred dollars. She'd be twenty-eight in a few months — how much younger did she want to look? "No, really, I just want the moisturizer. I can't really afford the rest right now."

"Oh, but you can," the woman crowed. "Just open a credit card account today and use it to make this purchase. You'll get five percent off and then you can pay for it over time."

By the time she paid it off it would be time to buy more. She was not going into debt to fight one little wrinkle. When she had two little wrinkles she might feel different. "Really, just the moisturizer."

The woman finally rang it up, after making Teresa wait while she recorded her list of recommended products — so next time they wouldn't have to start over. Teresa stopped in at Gloria Jean's for a latté, Godiva's for an ounce of chocolate-dipped white chocolate truffles, then set off at the fast-paced walk that would get her back to work sooner than the bus or Muni. She was glad the fog hadn't yet burned off for the afternoon. Summer in the city, cool and breezy as always.

The exercise made her brain function more clearly and she abruptly realized that she could wear the suit and shoes to her father's wedding at the end of next month. The pearl-gray suit would do nicely for a wedding; thank goodness she hadn't bought the black one. The weeks were flying by — time really did fly when you were having fun. She'd already redone all the note cards in the mustier exhibits, a task that had been waiting for attention for over three years. They even had color, courtesy of the inkjet she'd bought for them shortly after she started work. What a concept, Carla had said. Color in a museum.

She was serenely at work when Carla came looking for her. As usual, she arrived out of breath and stood poised to dash in any given direction at a moment's notice. "We're going to get a delivery in the next few days — approximately thirty small sculptures from an estate. It'll need to be sorted and cataloged."

Teresa leaned on the Egyptian papyrus display case. "It'll make a nice change. Is there anything of value?"

"There could be a Braque, which is why I said we'd value and catalog it for the family. They're big donors anyway. I wanted to tell you that a teacher from today's kid tour told me how much she appreciates the new note cards in here. She said she didn't know how the scroll ink was made and it was interesting to the kids."

"Just showing off my art school education."

"Keep it up." Carla twined a lock of platinum hair around her finger and leaned toward the exit as if she heard some silent call that needed her immediate attention. "You've been doing a great job."

"Thanks. I hope the board can be convinced to let me do a fabulous job on the database."

"Most of the board members are thrilled. Oh, and Eric has allowed as how he might be able to free up one of his assistants to collaborate. After all, they do know the fine arts collection best."

Teresa had wondered why Carla, who had only one

assistant — her — had been saddled with such a monumental task. She knew that Eric's assistants weren't sitting around eating bonbons, but there were three of them. "That will be great."

"Don't jump for joy yet. It seems the person who will help will also be doing the new Securi-tag inventory system."

"Oh. So I'll be helping out with that a little?"

"If it gets to be too much let me know. Actually, I do think this is a good idea. We don't want to finish our new database and have to go back and reenter the Securi-tag numbers or have a separate database for that. That would be counterproductive."

"I can see that. Well, I'll be glad for some help." So what if she spent time securing and coding the security tags; it was no big deal. It was the grunt work of running a museum and she'd expected to do a lot of it. One couldn't sit around all day looking at art. She would get to handle some of the finer pieces — it was something to be able to say you'd held a Man Ray or a Stuart Davis in your hands.

Carla headed for her office at a rapid pace. Teresa was just getting back to full concentration when her phone rang.

"I want you to meet me at that new bar I was telling you about," Vivian said.

"What new bar?"

"It's not new new, just new to us. The one where business types hang out."

"By that you mean older?"

"Maybe. How should I know?"

"Remind me why this is a good idea."

"Because we haven't met anyone new in at least three months. Hang on." She could hear Vivian telling someone that their brief would be out of the printer in five minutes. Apparently that was soon enough.

"Bars are never good places to meet anyone," Teresa observed.

"Well, hanging around at the library isn't working either. We need to branch out."

Teresa sighed. The truth of Vivian's statement was undeniable. She hadn't had a real date in way too long — just promises to meet for coffee that were canceled, or awkward arrangements to meet at the movies or a comedy club with everyone bringing a friend along just to make it clear it wasn't a date. Her first year of graduate school was the last time that anyone had made her heart, let alone other influential parts of her body, go *thump-thump*. "Okay, so where is this place?"

"Sort of between Noe Valley and the Castro —"

"So I can take a K, L or M, right?"

"If traffic is all messed up you could take the streetcar."

"Yeah, yeah. Let me write the address down."

After Vivian hung up, Teresa was vaguely depressed, and she'd been feeling so positive. Vivian hated being single with a passion, but Teresa didn't really know any other alternative. Her father had been a single parent and, honestly, this driving need to couple up seemed a little bit . . . stifling. Nobody stayed together these days, and coupling up early seemed like a sure way to break up. What if she had the opportunity to do a really interesting project on the other side of the country? Could she just pack up and go if she was living with someone?

So she didn't have Vivian's burning desire to find

Ms. Right, but lord knows she did need some more friends. It seemed like everyone from college was in either New York or Los Angeles, or so involved in their various installations and projects that they were never available for something fun. They weren't doing the 9-to-5 and were just starting their social day when Teresa was going to bed.

Vivian was a friend, but they would never be particularly close. All they had in common was their need to live someplace in San Francisco and the fact they were both gay. Vivian's income was a lot higher, but she sent a substantial sum home every month to her elderly parents. That made the amount they could afford to spend on housing just about the same. Vivian was a little too prim for Teresa's tastes. When one of them moved out, Teresa was willing to bet that Vivian wouldn't miss her foul mouth and love of loud action movies. But they got along, which was important between roomies.

Someone else who liked the things she liked, someone just to pal around with, that would be nice. She had wanted to camp out at Crissy Field to watch the Fourth of July fireworks last week, but no one would join her. Vivian didn't like sitting on the ground and other people at work had families. She looked down at her dusty Doc Martens and rumpled slacks. A businesswomen's bar, huh. There wasn't a chance anyone would take any notice of her.

Vivian had gone all out, which wasn't fair. Teresa almost hated to sit next to her, not for her own sake, but because she classed down Vivian's sheer black stockings, high heels and suit cut so short that Ally McBeal would blush.

Vivian waved with relief, so Teresa pushed her way to the bar. No one seemed to be paying particular attention to Vivian, which in Teresa's opinion made the women in the bar blind. Vivian had definite eye appeal — stylish clothes, tidy brown hair with attractive wisps around a pretty face. Her mannerisms were always demure, but she could turn on the sex appeal when she wanted to. She was only five-six, which in Teresa's opinion was the perfect height in a room full of women. Much better than her own five-nine. Really, there was nothing wrong with Vivian. Teresa could entertain lascivious thoughts if there was even the least amount of chemistry between them.

"Took you long enough," Vivian said. She patted the barstool she'd obviously been saving. "I'm getting the new-girl cold shoulder."

Teresa glanced around. Lots of couples — *sheesh* — and clusters of women who obviously already knew one another. "Is this where we want to be? A place with *Lace* in the name?" Over Vivian's shoulder she could see a small café, which was separated from the bar by a wall of open lattice. It was sort of cozy, but —

"What can I get you?"

Startled, Teresa said, "Um, how about a . . . well, do you have any house specialties?"

The bartender had wispy gray hair and a million-watt smile. "I make a Manhattan that leaves some women in tears —"

"Jill, you say that about all your women." The other bartender, who looked seventeen going on thirty, scooted past Jill and gave Teresa the once-over with an eyebrow wiggle. "What can I get you, hon?"

Jill rolled her eyes. "Okay, Sheila, but —" She glanced back at Teresa. "Her Manhattan is not as good as mine."

"But I make a killer Long Island iced tea." Sheila winked, so flirtatiously obvious that Teresa found it endearing. "Jill and I have an agreement. Under thirty is mine."

Teresa laughed. "Thank you for the compliment."

Vivian said, "Now that you're here I can go to the ladies' room and not lose our seats. I'll be right back."

"I'll take the Long Island iced tea," Teresa said. That appeared to be what Vivian was drinking.

Sheila was back in a minute with the drink. "I have a confession to make, hon."

"Yes?" Teresa sipped. Oh, that was tart, but the Triple Sec was so smooth by comparison. "This is great."

"Told you. Anyway, I'm just flirting with you because I want some inside information."

"Okay . . ." What the heck was she talking about?

"Is your friend, uh, one of us? She doesn't seem really responsive."

The light dawned. "Yes, most definitely, but she's very proper."

"Oh." Sheila gave the bar a swipe with the ubiquitous towel. "Maybe I came on a little strong."

"She has delicate sensibilities. But she is the sweetest person, and you'll always know exactly where you stand with her."

"She is the hottest woman to walk into this bar in about a year. Who isn't taken, I mean."

"You go, girl." Teresa sipped her drink again and

41

saw Sheila welcome Vivian back with a very warm smile.

"I bet you came here right from work," Sheila said. "Can I get you something to snack on beyond pretzels? Alcohol on an empty stomach can be disastrous." After protesting it was no trouble, Sheila disappeared in the direction of the kitchen and returned shortly with goat cheese on small rounds of toast and a small plate of strawberries dipped in chocolate.

"I have to hang out with you more often," Teresa said, her mouth full of the toast. She'd have a strawberry next. They were certainly a direct way to a lesbian's heart, Teresa thought.

"I don't know what you mean," Vivian retorted, but she lacked conviction, and a smile hovered around her mouth.

They danced when the floor filled a little — Sheila said she'd hold their barstools for them. She drifted off the floor when Vivian started dancing with a forty-ish size three. Teresa felt like an outsider. She lacked a suit and anything that amounted to cared-for hair, and her nails were down to the quick in several places. The dusty museum and the horrible hand soap had taken their toll.

She was finishing her drink and wondering if Vivian would kill her if she left when she heard Jill say to Sheila, "I'll be right back." Jill almost vaulted the bar to embrace someone who had just come in.

Intrigued, Teresa surreptitiously watched as the two women hugged for what seemed like an inordinately long time. When they separated Teresa nearly choked on her drink. It was *her*. The Queen of Mean. Looking slightly more approachable in slacks and what had to be a two-hundred-dollar sweater, she nonetheless still possessed that terrible core of condescension. Teresa felt like telling her off. But she hadn't had quite enough to drink and she'd been so much better about keeping her mouth shut lately. She was over it, anyway. She didn't need the satisfaction.

Jill accompanied Ms. Rayann Germaine, Queen of Mean, to a table in the café where a pale-looking woman was waiting. They, too, embraced for what seemed like ages, but Rayann's face was like stone when they parted. Geez, why did anybody waste any affection on this woman?

Without really deciding to, Teresa sidled up to the lattice wall, just on the other side of the table from where the two women sat. She couldn't help but wonder what Rayann was like when she was with a friend as opposed to a fresh-out-of-school employee she could bully.

". . . close to the end."

"I'm so sorry, Ray. Can I . . . tomorrow?"

The music changed to Randy Crawford's "Street Life" and it was harder to hear.

"Days, a week, who . . ."

". . . Dee wants to . . ."

Well that was frustrating. It wasn't until the song changed to a bluesy version of "Natural Woman" that she could hear again.

The friend was saying, "What kind of numb? Like anesthesia? Novocaine?"

"Not Novocaine."

"Why are you over here?" Vivian said, flushed and glistening — she *never* perspired, she'd told Teresa.

Teresa made a "be quiet" face at Vivian.

Vivian immediately disapproved. "Teresa, let's go

sit down again." She pulled Teresa away with a stern, "Eavesdroppers never hear good of themselves."

"That's her — the creative director bitch I told you about."

Vivian looked back. "Which one?"

"The dark hair."

"You didn't say how good-looking she is."

Teresa pronounced in her most prim manner, "Inner beauty is more important."

Vivian laughed, looking relaxed and happy for the first time in a while. "That's true until you're thirty-five."

Teresa let Vivian pull her away. "Oh yeah, that's ancient." She ducked Vivian's swat. "I gather you like this place."

"I do, indeed."

"The bartender likes you."

"I noticed. And over there is Kim, who works near me and would like to have lunch next Monday."

"You lucky girl. Can I go home now?"

"Actually, I'll go with you. Mission accomplished."

Kim and Sheila both waved as they left.

Teresa tried hard not to feel just a little bit lonely. She didn't want forever after, but a little here and now would be nice.

Judy's thoughtful gaze never left Rayann's face. "Why not Novocaine?"

"Novocaine is . . . there's no control. I wish I didn't feel anything, but I really don't want to lose control."

"Control has always been important to you, hasn't it?"

44

Rayann didn't want to get into it. There was just so much to explain, and Judy knew it all anyway. Why talk about what they both already knew? Why go into the past? "Let's not do the therapist-patient thing," she said finally.

Judy's look said, "You need help," but all she said was, "I'll try to remember that. We are supposed to be catching a bite to eat, after all."

Rayann wanted to say that she didn't need a therapist, she just needed her friends — Judy in particular — to know she was fine being left alone right now.

Lou, this is really shitty.

I know, came the reply.

She realized that Judy was watching her, the usual wrinkled frown creasing her forehead.

She wanted to say, "I'm okay," but Judy would not believe her. "So what's new with you?"

A vivid smile broke from Judy's worried face, catching Rayann by surprise. "Well, it's been thirteen weeks —"

"Has it? Thirteen weeks?" It was unthinkable that Louisa had been lying in that bed for thirteen weeks.

The smile disappeared, and Judy reached over to pat her hand. "It's weird, Ray. Remember when you called and I wasn't home? The day that — that Louisa was in the accident."

She would never forget. "Yeah?"

"Dee and I were at the clinic. You were so distracted I didn't want to bother you with the details of our latest attempt at fertility. And it's been thirteen weeks." Then Judy began to smile, and she nodded. "Yep."

"Oh my God. Finally!"

45

"Fourteen tries and I am due in the middle of January."

"Dee must be walking on air." Guilt stabbed at her for being so self-centered. Judy looked happy, but a little ashen around the edges. She should have noticed.

"I hope she is." Judy's therapist face was gone and it was just Judy, looking hurt and puzzled. "She's hardly said."

"But she was with you every step of the way. It was practically her idea."

"I know. But when that little stick turned blue she hardly reacted. I was so excited and she just froze. I've never seen her like this."

Rayann had. She'd been shopping with Dedric when Dedric had chased down a purse snatcher. "Cop face. She's scared shitless so she's got on her cop face."

Judy looked at her as if she'd grown a second head. "Good God. Out of the mouths of babes."

"I'm older than you, missy."

"I should have said amateurs. Good God, I never thought of that. She's afraid to show me she's scared."

"That's a butch for you."

"Tell me about it."

"I am so happy for you. I know it's been a real roller-coaster ride."

"I thought I was too old. Thirty-eight is late. Not too late, but late."

"And what's the significance of thirteen weeks?"

"The chance of spontaneous abortion drops significantly. The fetus has survived past the body's own DNA check, so to speak, and all systems are go."

"Jesus. A baby. Who'd have thunk it?"

"It's incredible, just incredible." Judy's expression

was positively beatific. "It won't be long until I feel it moving."

They managed to talk of inconsequential things after that, or the baby. Rayann was content to let the conversation drift just as long as they didn't talk about Louisa. Rayann had refused to leave the hospital for anything during visiting hours until Louisa had insisted with an emphatic "go" whispered through her aching throat.

Rayann knew they all just wanted her to have a little break, but even as they ate dessert she could feel the time slipping away. Time that would never come again, at no one's bidding. Every breath she took was a breath she didn't watch Louisa take. The beating of her own heart without the accompaniment of Louisa's monitor was solitary and meaningless, like one drum in the middle of the desert.

She drove Judy home, insisting that while a pregnant woman was not sick, she was a fool for turning down a ride. By the time she got to the hospital, visiting hours were almost over.

Her mother was in the chair next to Louisa's bed, reading aloud from *Pride and Prejudice*, Louisa's latest request. Rayann had a moment of vertigo, for she had not recognized her mother right away. How long had she looked so tired and strained? She knew she felt as if she'd aged a year for every week since the accident, but she had utterly failed to notice the effect on everyone else. Her mother looked . . . awful.

Her kiss of greeting was all the warmer. "Thanks for being here."

"You know you can't keep me away."

It was true. Her mother had been a daily visitor. Her mother's unique pain washed over her — she was losing not just her daughter's well-liked lover and partner, a daughter-in-law of sorts. She was also losing someone she'd come to regard as one of her dearest friends, a woman of nearly her own age with many similar likes and dislikes. She and Louisa had vacationed with her mother and second husband, Jim, several times. They'd seen Greece and Scotland together and been to countless concerts and plays. Watching her mother with Louisa had given Rayann new insights into her mother's character. She'd come to realize that she actually liked her mother and admired her devotion to friends and her ability to enjoy life.

She'd respected her mother's expertise in advertising so much that she'd decided to go back to the field. Ricki, a favorite customer at the bookstore, had eagerly agreed to part-time work, and Rayann's salary and bonuses had rapidly dispensed with the remaining mortgage, leaving Louisa with the best cash flow The Common Reader had ever had. After three years the bank balance was great, Ricki wanted more hours than ever and Louisa had finally admitted that she could relax a little.

Less time at the bookstore for Louisa was an impossibility when they lived right over it. It wasn't until Rayann found a suitable house within walking distance that Louisa had agreed to moving out of the only home she'd known for more than half her life. All that upheaval and mess — if they'd known they'd only share the new house for two months they would never have moved. If they'd never moved, Louisa's path to her favorite walk wouldn't have been altered. She would never have been on that street corner at that moment.

Rayann could not let go of the fact that moving had been her idea. She pushed back her turmoil and tried for a bright smile. "I have great news. Judy's pregnant," she told Louisa after she bent low to kiss her forehead.

She took one look at Louisa's drawn face and asked, "Have they been in to up your night dose?" Even as she asked the door opened and the nurse entered.

"I know I'm early," she said cheerily, "but doctor approved moving up the time a little." She glanced meaningfully at Rayann, then adjusted the IV drip.

It was the second time this week they'd moved back the timing of the morphine. The doctors were loath to increase the dosage because it virtually guaranteed that Louisa would become borderline comatose. She struggled so hard to communicate, to make the most of the times when she could listen and respond. But every window of lucidity was a journey in pain.

Someday it wasn't going to be worth it to Louisa anymore. *And what will I do then? What am I going to do when this is over?* Just as quickly, Rayann's guilty conscience demanded how she could even be thinking about that.

Her biggest enemy was guilt — guilt for not hoping, guilt for even thinking about a time after Louisa was gone. Guilt for believing the evidence the doctors shared with her regularly. After three months of hanging between better and worse, Louisa had finally turned the corner to worse. The lab tests showed that Louisa was wasting away every day, that kidney failure was imminent, that her damaged liver was producing an increasing level of toxins into her bloodstream. Finger pricks proved her pancreas was secreting insufficient insulin and Rayann believed the results. All of the medical science was at odds with any hope that she might have clung to, but she wasn't clinging, and for that she would never forgive herself.

Any one of Louisa's physical problems by itself might be overcome; combined they were devastating. Louisa had refused the transplants and various organ removals because they virtually assured her of spending the rest of her days tied to machines and bags that would prevent her from receiving the physical therapy and bone replacements she would need if she ever wanted to walk again.

Rayann believed that the end was near — she'd believed it from the start of these horrible months. Three months and counting. No one deserved this, she thought. She'd known it could be any day now every day since the accident, and her lack of faith ate at her.

The nurse and her mother were making small talk. There had been a time when she'd resented her mother's easy manner with just about everyone she met. When the nurse left, Rayann went back to her original news.

"Judy's baby is due in January and apparently Dee is really freaked out."

Louisa's fingers moved across the card, then she set it aside. Drawing a shallow breath, she whispered, "Happy for them. Kiss it for me. Don't think I'll be here."

"No, Lou," Rayann managed with a slight quaver. "Probably not. Jill sends her love."

Louisa smiled and her eyelids fluttered. The morphine had kicked in. "Tell Jill . . . same." She drew another shallow breath. "Ann?"

Her mother leaned into Louisa's line of sight. "I'm just going."

"Mr. Darcy is a fool," Louisa managed, then coughed.

"I can't wait to start the next chapter," her mother said with the flash of eagerness she showed when she and Louisa discussed anything. "I wish I'd read it before."

Louisa was nodding off. Her mother dabbed a tissue at her nose and slipped out as Rayann kissed the parched lips tenderly, then offered water. Louisa drank briefly, then slept.

The door opened again, this time admitting her favorite resident, the very first doctor she and Teddy had talked to. Dr. Kiung had a well of genuine sympathy that the rigors of resident medicine hadn't yet drained.

"I waited too long," he said, glancing at the sleeping Louisa. "I was hoping to catch her awake while you were here."

"What is it?" Rayann knew she should brace herself for bad news, but she didn't have any bracing left.

He sat down and talked quietly. "You can't tell in this light, but her skin is tinting orange. That's an indication of jaundice. I expect the blood test we did this afternoon to confirm that diagnosis."

"What does that mean?"

"The blood test will tell us if the jaundice is being caused by a virus, like viral hepatitis, or by an obstruction that is allowing the pigments in the liver's bile to reach the skin. That's where the color comes from."

"So what will you do?" The question came out automatically. Rayann felt as if she was mouthing lines from a script.

"If it's an obstruction, an operation is the only way to fix it."

"She won't survive an operation. Maybe a month ago she might have. And I don't think she'll agree anyway."

He nodded with a flicker of a smile. "Given that her first instructions to me were 'Get this fucking tube out of my throat,' I think you're right. And you're also right — it's highly unlikely she'd survive the operation anyway. I can't believe she's still alive, frankly." He cleared his throat. "Anyway, if the jaundice is caused by a virus we can treat it, but the treatments can be unsuccessful. But I think we'll discover it's a blockage."

"When will you know?"

"Tomorrow morning."

"And if she won't have the operation?"

"A matter of days. We'll be barely able to keep her comfortable, considering her morphine dosage now."

Rayann said slowly, "So what you're saying is that if the jaundice is being caused by liver failure or a blockage and she doesn't have an operation, she's going to need more morphine to be comfortable until she . . . dies. And so the brief periods of consciousness she's been having are just about over."

"Yes." He blinked back tears and she realized she didn't know his first name. She had become so self-centered. "If she declines the operation, I would say good-bye."

"Thank you for telling me. I'll let her son know, too. I know she won't agree to the operation." She looked at Louisa's profile. "She's said her good-byes, most of them."

She turned off the bedside light and sat in the dark. The heart monitor bleeped. She'd always thought it was off-key, somehow.

She shied away from accepting that she might have only one or two more chances to tell Louisa how much she loved her. Finding the words was hard. A thousand words could not begin to describe the way her life molded to Louisa's, the way her soul had dreamed once it had filled with Louisa's love. That Louisa was dying was incomprehensible because her heart would not let go. She would never let go.

4

Teddy signed the paperwork the administrative aide proffered and then handed the clipboard to Rayann. "I still feel this isn't necessary. She's quite able to decide for herself."

Rayann looked down at the little space while the aide mouthed something about hospital policy. By signing she was adding her consent to lack of treatment as specified by Louisa, and she was admitting she understood the serious consequences of not accepting the advised treatment. The consequence was liver failure in anywhere from twelve to forty-eight hours.

She didn't understand any of it. The world was a shadow and nothing had any substance. She'd achieved the numb state that she'd told Judy she needed.

The pen moved across the paper, leaving blue marks against white.

I'm letting you die. I expected you to go first, but not like this.

I didn't expect this either.

Teddy shook her gently. "It's what she wants."

"I know." She wanted to be angry at the hospital for making her sign the paper, for making Teddy sign it. Did they really make adult children sign something like this if there was a spouse? But she didn't want to sign it either. She didn't want the responsibility.

The aide took the clipboard out of her hands, tugging it a little when her fingers wouldn't unclench. The knifing pain in her heart was almost as bad as that first day, when the doctor had written *DNR* on Louisa's chart.

"I'm very sorry for the pain your mother is going through." The aide's words were automatic. She'd probably said them hundreds of times. Only after she was gone did Rayann realize the aide had been speaking to her, not Teddy.

She boiled with rage for a long minute, then it subsided as quickly as it had come, leaving her shaking. Teddy made her sit down.

Even at the end people did not want to accept what the chart said — that she was Louisa's lover, not her daughter. She didn't know if they refused to accept it because they were both women, or because she was so much younger than Louisa, nearly thirty years. It didn't matter.

Louisa hovered at the edge of consciousness. She tried to say something, so Rayann leaned down, wanting to climb into the bed with her, but being jostled would only cause Louisa more pain. Despite the maximum dose of morphine she'd been given, Louisa had been in tears after the morning's therapeutic massage to stave off bedsores.

"I'm here, darling," Rayann said.

"I love you." The whisper didn't convey the Garbo-esque tone of Louisa's voice, but Rayann heard it in her heart. "I just wanted to say it again."

Rayann delicately stroked Louisa's cheek. Her eyes saw the distinctive orange-yellow tint, but her mind didn't register it. "I know." A thousand words churned inside her, but she could only manage a few past her choking throat. "I count the ways, every day," she whispered.

Louisa tried to nod. "Thank you for not arguing about operations, machines."

She had wanted to argue, to scream and fight, but she knew it was pointless. Once Louisa's mind was made up there was no changing it. It was that way in everything. "It's your choice, darling. I would never take it from you."

For a moment Louisa's eyes flickered with desire, and Rayann felt her body responding. One last time — God, what she would give for one last time. She instantly hated herself for thinking about her physical needs.

Louisa whispered, "Kiss me. I love you."

It tasted of tears and yesterday, and memories of

longing and fulfillment, a twining dance of desire as pleasurable as satisfaction.

"No tears," Louisa said. She closed her eyes. "Promise me . . ."

"What?"

"It's a cliché."

"Can't have that," Rayann managed to tease. She was rewarded by the glimmer of a smile. It was enough.

"Don't chain up your heart. I loved again after Chris . . . didn't think I would. Wasn't looking for you. You can, too. Promise me." Louisa's voice was getting thready. Rayann offered water and waited while Louisa drank.

"I promise," she said. What was one little lie if it would give Louisa some peace? "Teddy's here."

"Please."

They'd gotten very good at jumping over useless conversation. No need for Louisa to say "good" or "how nice." Just "please" for "I want to talk to him."

She made room for Teddy and looked unseeingly at the O'Keeffe prints she'd hung around the room. She even heard something like a laugh from Teddy. Louisa should by all rights be exhausted, but she was clinging to awareness as the closest family and friends came to say good-bye. There would be no funeral, just a family-only burial. What was the point, Louisa had wanted to know, of everyone saying nice things after she died? Why not say them while they had the chance? No funeral, but a party was planned. Louisa had even chosen the music.

While Nancy, an old friend who ran Oakland's women's center, was visiting, Teddy stood by Rayann at the window.

He spoke quietly so neither Louisa nor Nancy could overhear. "I heard from the trucking company lawyers again today. They've upped the settlement offer."

She detested all mention of the lawsuit. She hadn't wanted to sue, but Teddy had insisted if only for the symbolic gesture. It was the litigator in him, she supposed. Louisa had decided to let Teddy pursue it on her behalf, saying the money could go to her favorite charities, which would be something good from something bad. The company had known the driver had a history of drunk driving but hired him anyway. "Can we not talk about it now?"

"I don't want to, but the offer expires tomorrow and I'm negligent if I don't tell you," Teddy explained. "Their timing is pretty awful."

"Let it expire." The company obviously wanted it over and done with but right now Rayann would not give them any satisfaction.

"That's what I thought." He didn't say any more, but Rayann had no trouble following his legal reasoning. They would gain much more in a settlement after Louisa died and all the beneficiaries, including Louisa's numerous charities, would be better off.

She felt sick to her stomach. The smell of antiseptic was making her gag.

She didn't deserve this. Louisa didn't deserve this.

Late in the afternoon Louisa's strength gave out. Rayann knew the moment it happened because one moment Louisa had been listening intently to *Pride and Prejudice,* and the next her eyes were closed. Her hands went limp.

After a minute the respiration monitor blared, but

Louisa didn't move. The nurse came in, checked Louisa's pulse, then the machines. Dr. Kiung did the same thing two minutes later.

"I'm going to administer an APNEA test," he told the nurse, who took the chart and nodded. He flicked light into Louisa's eyes and pricked different parts of her body to see if any pain was registering. Louisa didn't move.

Rayann was breathing hard. She felt like a marathon runner in the twenty-fifth mile. Her mother came to stand next to her. She clutched the book she'd been reading aloud as if it could give her comfort.

Dr. Kiung made some low-voiced observations to the nurse, then turned to them. "There is still pupil activity, and I think her current state has more to do with the morphine than anything else. I mean that she hasn't had a stroke or seizure. She's in a state of collapse."

There was a long silence, then her mother asked quietly, "Will she regain consciousness again?"

Dr. Kiung shook his head. "I seriously doubt it." He swallowed hard. "And I can't say it would be a good thing for her if she did."

"We understand," her mother said. "Thank you."

Teddy was shaking; Rayann could sense it. There was a knock on the door and Joyce came in, stopping short after a quick look at Louisa. Teddy went to her without a word while Rayann accepted her mother's tight embrace.

"I'm so sorry, honey, so sorry."

They waited together, the four of them. Joyce made a quick phone call to have a friend keep Tucker for the night, then they waited. The dinner hour came and went. Her mother called Jim to let him know she would be at the hospital all night if need be.

They didn't turn on the lights after the sun set, so Rayann did not know how long Louisa's fingers had been moving when she finally noticed it. She hurried to the bedside and leaned down, her head on the pillow. "I'm here."

Louisa's lips moved, as if she was dreaming. The heart monitor stopped beeping. The horrible flat tone was worse than any TV show could make it.

Teddy was jamming the nurse call button, but the door was already opening. The lights came on as two nurses entered quickly. They efficiently took vitals and cleared space next to the bed. Dr. Kiung, looking very weary, came a few moments later and stopped the nurses.

"She's DNR. Cancel the code blue, please."

Rayann turned her face into her mother's shoulder.
It's not you.
Not anymore, my love.

Dr. Kiung clenched his fists as if to keep his hands still. After a few minutes he checked Louisa's pupils, then said softly to one nurse, "Time of death is nine-fourteen." He turned off the heart monitor and only then did Rayann hear everyone else's tears.

After months of crying, her well was dry. She was the only one who didn't cry.

"To Louisa!"

Teresa watched everyone in the Lace Place bar

raise their glass. She turned to Vivian. "It looks like some sort of party. Maybe we're here on a bad night."

Even as she said it, the bartender, Jill, was hurrying over. "I'm sorry there's not much room in the bar tonight, and there won't be any dancing. We're having a wake. The café is open if you're hungry. We can bring drinks in there, if you'd like."

"I'm starving," Vivian said. She looked disappointed, too.

Jill showed them to a table. By peeking through the lattice wall Teresa could see the "mourners." They all looked like they were having a good time. She noticed a blow-up of a woman's photograph — older, probably late sixties. But very . . . handsome. Gorgeous hair lifted in a brisk wind, like sewing silks of silver and black. Teresa wondered what she had died of.

As she glanced at the other people in the bar, she saw one woman who tickled her memory. The redhead next to the woman was a stranger — she'd have remembered the thick, Titian hair. She pointed her out to Vivian.

"Oh my," Vivian said. "No, I don't think she was here before. I wouldn't have forgotten."

They ordered their dinner, but it was hard to talk with the increasing hubbub in the bar. More toasts to the departed Louisa were given. Teresa's cobb salad was good, if a tad simple, but it filled the hungry spot.

"So much for my meeting anyone," Teresa said. She indicated her suit and heels. "I'm as dressed up as I'll ever get."

"You looked great for your big board meeting. I'm glad it went well."

"I'm really glad we got the money. It wasn't much.

I was scared I wouldn't present it very well, but it seemed to go okay. A couple of board members even said thank you — oh, now I remember."

"Remember what?"

Teresa quickly swallowed. "The woman next to the redhead. She was here with the creative director from hell."

"Haven't you gotten over that yet?" Vivian delicately dabbed away a smidgen of dressing from the corner of her mouth. Teresa couldn't believe her lipstick wasn't even smudged. If she wore lipstick it got all over everything.

"Of course. I just couldn't remember where I'd seen her before."

"You were oil and water. You should put it behind you."

"I have," Teresa insisted.

"That's good," Vivian said, "because she's right over there." She pointed with her fork.

Teresa had to look twice. Rayann Germaine seemed dwarfed by a broad-shouldered man sitting next to her. Teresa remembered the way Rayann's vivid personality had seemed like an assault. That was all turned around now. She was not just cold, but frozen. All the vitality and life around her seemed to get sucked into her stillness, leaving her wholly unaffected. Even when she spoke she seemed silent. It reminded Teresa a little of DaVinci's *Last Supper*. Everyone else was talking and eating, but Rayann, like DaVinci's Christ, was focused inward as if contemplating an inevitable sadness.

Teresa noticed the redhead helping the pale woman next to her up — ah, the pale woman was in a maternity blouse, which probably accounted for her pallor. The redhead briefly rested her hand on the other woman's slightly swollen belly. Doing the lesbian mommy thing, apparently.

"You're staring," Vivian said.

"Sorry." She took another bite of her cobb salad and grimaced when she got more blue cheese than she liked at any one time.

Vivian had apparently seen the two women as well, because she asked, "Have you ever thought about having kids?"

"Not really. My dad would be thrilled no matter how they arrived. But I think his soon-to-be son-in-law has two kids, which takes the pressure off me."

"Used to be, just being a lesbian you got to walk away from that kind of pressure."

Teresa grinned. "More choices — I didn't really need them." Vivian looked pensive, so Teresa asked, "What about you?"

"I'd love to have a big family. Lots of kids, at least three. I have five brothers and sisters and I miss the closeness of family. That's why I broke up with Tamala last year. She was dead set against it. I hear the clock ticking, but I don't think I can do it all by myself." She sipped her water, then studied the glass after she set it down. "All my brothers and sisters have kids and none of them has two cents to rub together. Which leaves me helping out mom and dad because I don't have kids. And if I had kids I wouldn't be able to help mom and dad anymore. My family is accepting of my being gay, but I know they feel I don't really have a life. So I can afford to be the major support. If I lived closer I'd be the one stopping by twice a week to make sure they have groceries, but my two sisters take care of that. I just pay the bill."

As an only child with a hale and hearty father, Teresa found it hard to relate. "I know it's not easy. But I don't know about having kids. I like my solitude."

"Give it a few more years, you won't."

"You talk like you are so much older than I am."

"Six long years."

Teresa shrugged. "What's six years, here or there?"

Vivian wrinkled her not-in-the-least-bit-pointy nose, which Teresa envied. "They haven't happened to you yet. You're still on the verge."

"Verge of what?"

"Life. Whatever life has in store. This is when you find out what you're really made of and what you're not. You'll be into your life before you know it, and nothing will be the way you thought it would be."

Teresa wanted to say, "For you, not for me," but for once her mouth knew when to stay shut. She knew that Vivian had wanted to be a lawyer but failed to pass the bar in several tries. She had also discovered she couldn't handle the long hours and stress. Instead she was a paralegal and highly valued precisely because she did not want to be a lawyer. "Will it be so awful?"

Vivian lost her cynical edge with a sudden grin. "Not if you learn to accept Plan B with grace and style."

Teresa laughed. "Well, I managed one Plan B already."

"And it worked out for the best, didn't it?"

"Your advice and wisdom far outweigh my own."

"Plan A is leaving." Vivian nodded in the direction of the bar.

Teresa glanced over. The man was hugging Rayann. Another woman held her coat, as if waiting for a small child to get ready to go. She had some kind of magic, that woman. The whole world doted on her, apparently.

She would never understand it.

"Shall we call it a night?" Vivian sighed. "I had hoped for more, I must say. Kim hasn't called in two weeks so I think we might be fizzling."

"Sorry. I'm a poor substitute for romance and passion."

"You're okay in your own way," Vivian allowed.

"The feeling is mutual. I want to walk over to the bookstores in the Castro, though. If I can't dance I may as well find something to read. I need something for the flight, anyway."

"I think I'll go home," Vivian said. "It's probably just as well we can't dance. I'm more tired than I thought I was."

They parted at the door, Vivian turning toward the Muni station while Teresa set off uphill. She immediately wished she was wearing something other than the black pumps Vivian had voted for. She was going to get a blister.

The direct route up the steeper hills was shorter, and she got to the Castro main drag before her feet gave up. The next Muni stop was also much closer.

A slow-walking woman ahead of her turned into a bar and Teresa did a double take. Wasn't that Rayann? Going into one of the men's bars?

Curious, and knowing it was absurd, she followed. A wall of disco music assaulted her when she opened the door. The men in the bar quickly dismissed her, and she saw Rayann at the far end, talking to the bartender. The bartender brought her a drink and she downed half of it in a gulp.

Was *that* the woman's problem? Drinking? That could account for the Jekyll and Hyde.

It was more than just her leftover hurt feelings that made her force her way through the crowd to the other end of the bar. Just once, she thought, just once, she would like Rayann Germaine to look at her, really look at her, and take note of the fact that she was a human being. Just once.

The two men on the other side of Rayann were getting hot and heavy. In a few minutes they left by the back door, which opened onto the alley behind the bar. Teresa slipped onto the deserted barstool next to Rayann.

The bartender brought Rayann another drink. Teresa leaned forward so he could hear her. "I'll have one of those, too."

It was a gin and tonic. Rayann didn't look up from her contemplation of the glass until Teresa quite un-accidentally bumped her.

"Sorry," she shouted in Rayann's ear.

"No problem."

Two drinks later, all Teresa could think was, "This is stupid." Rayann was deep into her own thoughts and two drinks ahead of her. Even if Teresa did get her attention, she was clearly in no condition to talk.

Did she really want to talk? No, all she wanted was acknowledgment. A look of recognition. Teresa realized the gin was having an effect on her own ability to think, but she was still clear on what she wanted. Rayann Germaine had delivered the cruelest insult of all — she had failed to recognize that Teresa was even there. She wasn't leaving this bar until she had some satisfaction.

The bartender brought her another gin and tonic, but Teresa hadn't ordered it yet. She waved it away, but Rayann signaled for it.

"I'll take it."

The bartender shouted over the music, "You driving?"

Rayann shook her head and then fished clumsily in her coat pocket. She held up a Muni pass.

The bartender shrugged and said, "It's your last, then."

Rayann managed to fumble her wallet out of her pants pocket and handed over a couple of bills to settle her tab. Teresa decided it was high time she did the same. Getting drunk was not why she was here. She pocketed her change and watched Rayann steadily drain the gin and tonic.

Last chance, she thought. Teresa leaned very close. Too close to be ignored. "Would you like to dance?"

Rayann's eyes were half-closed, but she nodded. Teresa stood up, but Rayann stayed on her barstool, just opening her arms like she was going to dance while seated. Before Teresa knew it, Rayann's head was nestled under her chin. She was tingling all over. It was a very nice kind of tingling, like she hadn't felt in a long time.

"This isn't quite what I had in mind," Teresa said, more to herself than to Rayann.

Rayann looked up dreamily. "Just what did you have in mind?"

She hardly hesitated. In a heartbeat the desire was formed and acted on. She pressed her lips to Rayann's, and when she found a soft and eager welcome, she intensified her pressure until Rayann's lips parted.

A part of her, growing smaller by the moment, was not proud of what she was doing. But mostly she couldn't stop. She changed her position, stepped between Rayann's parting legs and cupped Rayann's face in her hands.

When Teresa pulled away Rayann was gasping. Her eyes were closed, and she reached for Teresa again. "I've missed you."

What the hell? She started to push Rayann back, but found Rayann's hands inside her jacket, slowly pulling her blouse out of her skirt. "Don't do that. Not here."

Rayann smiled sexily and Teresa felt another jolt of desire. "Only your mouth is saying no."

Teresa arched her back as warm fingertips found her bare skin. She remembered the door to the alley. "This way."

Rayann followed, her step uncertain but eager. Once they were outside, she pulled Teresa against her so that Teresa had her pinned to the wall. Her mouth was like a fire of longing, burning Teresa's lips and tongue. She was drawing Teresa's hands under her sweater and in the next moment undoing Teresa's blouse buttons.

Teresa wanted to go on, every part of her did. It would not be the first time she'd done something so stupid. But it seemed very wrong.

"It's been too long," Rayann whispered, and Teresa realized what was wrong. Rayann had no idea who she was, or rather, Rayann was drunkenly pretending she was someone else.

Her hands had found their way to Rayann's full

and soft breasts and Teresa's resolve to end things before it went any further crumbled. Rayann's fingers were inside her shirt, hurriedly fumbling their way under Teresa's bra.

It felt too good to stop. The next kiss gave her vertigo and abruptly she found herself with her back against the wall.

"Your turn for once," Rayann whispered. Her hands were under Teresa's skirt now.

The warm pressure against her crotch was delicious, but it jolted Teresa to where she was. She grabbed Rayann's arms. "We can't do this here."

"Take a walk on the wild side," Rayann protested. She tried to engage another kiss, but Teresa held her off. Then her eyes snapped open.

"Oh God," Rayann gasped, then she stumbled to the other side of the alley and was spectacularly sick.

Teresa felt the cold night air on her breasts. Her entire body was like a vibrating bowstring. She pulled her bra down, buttoned up and then went to help Rayann.

Rayann gasped, between heaves, "Leave me alone. Just leave me alone."

Teresa let her mouth have its way. "Fuck you. I just want to help." She stormed back into the club and stood there feeling guilty and enraged and really, really frustrated. Finally, she picked up a stack of napkins and went back outside. "Here," she snapped.

"Thanks," Rayann mumbled. She wiped her mouth and hands, then leaned weakly against the wall. After a minute she pushed herself upright, wrapped her coat tightly around her waist and walked down the alley toward the street.

Teresa stood there with her mouth open. What the

fuck had just happened? You know what just happened, she told herself. That bitch got one look at you and she puked, that's what happened. You were never real to her. That's been the whole problem all along.

She walked in the opposite direction to the Muni station, feeling as if she really wanted another drink. But she'd obviously had enough and there was no way this evening was going to end on an up note. She did remember to stop at the bookstore for something to read on the flight to Vegas.

It wasn't until she was packing the following morning that she realized she'd bought one of those true love romances where girl meets girl, girl has fabulous sex with girl, and girls settle down in the suburbs to live happily ever after.

Well, it would be good for a laugh. It was certainly not the story of her life. And as for Ms. Rayann Germaine — Teresa pictured her trapped in a Hieronymous Bosch painting. Her mind's eye painted the passionate mouth and trembling skin writhing in Bosch's purgatory. Writhing in torment and nothing else.

5

Rayann quickly regretted opening her eyes. Behind her closed lids she tried to decide where she was. She remembered the woman — had she gone home with her? She wasn't wearing anything.

She risked another peek and was much relieved to recognize her old bedroom. She was at her mother's house. Now she vaguely remembered giving the cab driver her mother's address because it was closer and she needed a bathroom as soon as possible. Jim had been the one to let her in. Her clothes were neatly folded on the chair, so her mother had at some point helped her get into bed.

Her head ached too much to move.

What had she been thinking? What had she been trying to achieve? Orgasm with some stranger, as if that could ever be enough? How could she even have contemplated it?

Even now she could feel that woman's body against hers — but was she really remembering that, or just longing for Louisa, wishing she could make love with her one last time.

I want you, I'll never stop.

Behind her eyelids she could see Louisa giving her the look that said, "I'm taking you to bed the moment we're alone." It had always left her trembling.

She wanted to run away from her memories.

I loved you for more than the sex, you know that. Please tell me you know that.

Softly, comfortingly, the reply came. *I know.*

Rayann managed to sit up. It didn't seem right that all she could think about, all she could remember was the sex. The accident hadn't just taken away the best lover she had ever had, it had taken away the laughter and shared joys, the morning coffee and teasing banter. She'd lost all of Louisa, not just her body.

In the two weeks since Louisa's death, Rayann had longed for Louisa's body. The longing fueled her guilt. She hadn't loved Louisa enough, not nearly enough.

Her mother had left a note on the bedside table. She and Jim had left for a wedding reception but would be home in time for an early supper, and would she please consider staying. They were probably worried about her, just like Judy was. She wished everyone would stop worrying. Of course, showing up drunk and sick in the middle of the night wasn't going to inspire confidence.

She found aspirin, showered, and resolved to show her mother and Jim that she was fine. She could hold herself together long enough to do that. She would prove to them that she was not having a breakdown, that she was getting on with her life. She knew that Tony Hand was waiting for her call, eager to hear that she was on her way back to work. But she just couldn't take that step. Going back to work would mean leaving Louisa behind. It would mean admitting the impossible had happened.

You're not dead. You're not gone.

As she brushed out her hair, Rayann took stock of the ravages that four months of grief and anger had taken. All that time spent waiting for Louisa to die, and now two weeks of living with the reality of it. Her skin was dry and brittle, her eyelashes thin, her eyebrows overgrown, her hair limp and streaked with more gray. She'd aged ten years. She was the epitome of a "before" picture in an advertisement. But she had no idea what an "after" picture might look like without Louisa there, holding her, making her think, giving her courage.

She'd slept past noon, and shaking off hangover lethargy was hard. She found a recent copy of *Advertising Age* in her mom's office and took it into the backyard. The dappled August sunlight made her drowsy. She rocked in the hammock and relived the day she'd met Louisa, agreed to live in her house and work in the bookstore. Remembering that day made her think of Michelle, the faithless lover that Rayann had bolted from, right into Louisa's life. God, she hadn't thought about Michelle in ages. What a pointless relationship that had been. Michelle's income had given her the freedom to pursue sculpture and teaching art. But she wasn't cut out to be an artist. She forgot who she had said it to, but she really did like advertising.

The whir of the garage door brought her out of her doze and she tried to look energetic and alert when Jim and her mother came in the house.

"You look a little better than you did last night," Jim observed, giving her a quick hug.

"I feel better. My stomach's still telling me that I had twice a few too many."

Her mother glanced around the kitchen. "You haven't eaten anything, have you?"

"Not yet — I wasn't sure what dinner plans were and didn't want to spoil my appetite."

Her mother let the lie pass and offered to make coffee. "Or we could hop back in the car and go out to eat. Reception appetizers and sugary cake always makes me hungry for dim sum. We'll be way ahead of the rush at my favorite place on Webster."

Rayann pressed a hand to her stomach. "As long as there aren't any chicken feet I'll be fine. Don't you guys want to change?"

Her mother would have skipped it, but Jim quickly said, "I'm dying to." He disappeared upstairs.

Her mother picked up the copy of *Advertising Age* Rayann had abandoned on the counter. "Are you heading back to work soon?"

The question made Rayann angry, and she knew it was irrational. Her mother wasn't being deliberately cruel. When she didn't answer, her mother put the magazine down and crossed the room to draw Rayann to the table.

Once they were seated, she fixed Rayann with her direct gaze. As the years passed, looking into her mother's face was more like looking into a mirror. But she'd never have that piercing gaze, Rayann thought. Her mother was so much stronger than she was.

"You're too much like me," her mother said. "You don't like getting advice any better than I do. But out of everyone you know, I'm the only one who understands how hard it is to go on."

Rayann bit her lower lip. Only after Louisa had died did Rayann realize she had a common bond with her mother, who had lost her life mate, Rayann's father, to a heart attack. Ten years ago she'd still thought her mother cold, a belief that dated from her father's funeral, when her mother had not cried.

She hadn't cried at Louisa's burial. At times of extreme grief they both went cold.

Her mother's eyes were filled with tears now. "I know what you're going through. The disbelief, the anger — God, the guilt. Do you know how many nights I went to sleep asking myself if I pushed your father into working too hard? If I encouraged him to have one too many cheesecake desserts?"

"He was perfectly fit, Mom — it was congenital, the failure. I had all those tests to make sure it hadn't been passed on."

"I blamed myself anyway. If I'd loved enough, cared enough, it wouldn't have happened."

Rayann closed her eyes. Although she knew her mother had gone through the same loss, she rejected the idea that anybody could understand. Her guilt was different — she needed only to have lingered for one more kiss that morning, or called when she got to work. Anything to put Louisa one minute later on her walk.

Her mother patted her hand. "If you want to talk, I'm here, sweetie. And even though you won't believe me, life goes on. It has to. That's what life is — a force that cannot stand still. Moving on does not mean you loved her less."

"I know that." Intellectually, she did. Her heart didn't believe it for a second.

They sat in silence for a moment, then Jim came into the kitchen. He put his arm around Rayann's shoulders on the way to the car, as affectionate with her as he was with his own son. Dinner was light-hearted on the surface, but Rayann knew she had to face going home when it was over. Tomorrow would come and she would have to fill another day.

I miss you.
Of course.

Las Vegas was a trip. The fantastical hotels and casinos, surrounded by fountains and pools all at odds with the blazing desert heat, made Teresa shake her head. What had Carla called it? A city built by losers. She'd read that there wasn't enough water to support the city anymore, and yet she could see two more large casinos under construction.

The whimsy of the architecture — faux Roman next to an Egyptian oasis across from a circus big tent, all crowned with neon marquees — was garish in the hot afternoon sun. The sheer excess of it was the worst of

American culture, but it succeeded so well at excess that she gawked along with the other people in the shuttle.

The shuttle driver regaled everyone with stories of big wins. She learned that the Hello Dollar slot machine was due to hit and gathered she should hurry down with her silver dollars to get lucky. The heat slapped her as she stepped from the shuttle. Moments later she was engulfed by the chill of the hotel air conditioning. She glanced over her shoulder — five feet from the door and she couldn't tell if it was day or night. The ringing of slot machines filled her ears. Carla's offhand remarks about the psychology of casinos was taking some of the excitement out of her first experience.

In her room she abandoned her leggings and T-shirt and shrugged into a short skirt and lightweight top that was better suited to the heat and more presentable. It was so cold inside she could wear the cute little jacket that went with the skirt. She didn't want to embarrass her father by looking like a scruffy student at dinner. She was an assistant curator. She stood up straight, then relaxed. She was also on vacation — the first vacation of her working life.

She grabbed her room key, wallet and the five bucks in quarters she'd been given when she checked in. No cost to the hotel — they knew the quarters were headed right for their slot machines. She'd have just enough time to lose them all before she joined up with the others at the rooftop restaurant.

She had put all of the hotel's quarters into a machine, then dropped another twenty quarters of her own when the machine began ringing wildly and coins clinked out. She was just thinking that gambling was easy when she realized her so-called jackpot was four dollars. Crud.

She was not cut out for gambling. You're too suspicious, she told herself. She changed her quarters to bills and headed for the elevator to the restaurant.

When the doors opened at the top floor her father was there. She landed in his arms with a banshee whoop that would have left Vivian's sensibilities fainting.

"It's so *good* to see you," they said in unison.

"You look great, punkin!"

She tugged on the beard he'd been cultivating the last two years. "Still growing this sad excuse for facial hair?" He looked great, too. Love agreed with him.

"I had it trimmed for the occasion," he said with mock dignity.

"What, with baby nail clippers? That took all of two seconds."

"You have no respect for your elders."

"I do so. I just don't have any —"

"— respect for you," he chimed in. "Ha ha ha. Mel and Ken are at the table. Come on. Behave."

She'd met Melanie last Christmas, when she'd flown down to L.A. to spend winter break with her father. She'd liked the older woman well enough, but would have made more of an effort to be welcoming if she'd realized Melanie meant so much to her dad. Melanie had a steady, gray gaze that shone with humor. She was carefully made up, but not at all in the same league as Vivian in terms of fussy precision. Her lightweight knit set made Teresa very glad she had taken the time to wear something nice.

"You remember Mel, of course. And this is Ken."

Ken, Melanie's son, rose to shake her hand. He

was roughly her own age and several inches taller. Teresa immediately disliked him. Don't be silly, she chastised herself. First impressions can be very wrong. So his handshake was a little damp and limp and his mouth turned down slightly with an air of long-suffering. So his eyes held none of his mother's humor. He had a nice mom — how bad could he be?

Her father held her chair for her, then said with a laugh, "I almost introduced Reese as my best girl. But that was going to get me into trouble."

"You're going to have to come up with another way to introduce me, Dad." She grinned at Melanie. "He can be a little slow."

"Reese?"

"Yeah, Dad?" She studied her menu.

"Shup."

"Okay," she said, adding in a stage whisper, "At least until after the wedding."

Melanie laughed. Now Teresa remembered one of the reasons she'd liked Melanie — she found as much to laugh about as her father did.

The waiter filled her wineglass and Ken cleared his throat. "I want to propose a toast," he said formally.

Ken, Teresa decided, did not laugh enough. Maybe she could loosen him up.

"To my mother," he continued.

"Hear, hear," her father said. He was watching Ken indulgently. He must have some good qualities, Teresa decided.

"And to Alan," Ken went on.

"Hear, hear." Teresa tapped her knife on her wineglass for extra effect. Ken stared at her until she stopped. "Sorry," she muttered. "I come from a long line of interrupters." She sat on her hands.

"You're obviously blessed to have found each other," Ken said. "May you find joy in your life together and God's gift of happiness."

Teresa's inner alarms went off. She was too gay not to worry a bit when strangers said something religious. *God, if you do exist, please let him not be a Lou Sheldon supporter. I don't really need any cosmic jokes, okay?*

"Thank you, sweetie," Melanie said.

The restaurant was mellow and the service attentively slow. Her father and Melanie did most of the talking when they weren't dancing.

She and Ken ate their desserts while Melanie and her father foxtrotted to their hearts' content. After two minutes of silence, Teresa leaned forward with what she hoped was charm and asked Ken what he thought of Las Vegas.

"I had read they were trying to make the Strip more family-friendly," he said. "I don't see it. I can't think of a single way that gambling could support a family's values."

"What if the parents are bookies?" The look on Ken's face made her quickly say, "I'm joking, of course."

"What were your first impressions of Las Vegas?" He was obviously just being polite.

"That it was hot. I mean, that was my very first impression. This is my first vacation since I left school, so I'm feeling very easy to please. I was amused by the architecture."

"Your father said you work in a museum."

She nodded. "It's not one of the big ones, but the collection is unique. We specialize in small art — small sculpture, work on paper. Preliminary sketches, early works. We also have one of the best collections of Man Ray." Ken looked a little dazed. "Not very many people know his work. He was an American contemporary of Marcel Duchamp — you have probably seen his *Nude Descending a Staircase*." Thank God, a small nod.

"Man Ray is primarily known for his dada works and for the innovation of spray-gun painting . . . um, and he did a lot of photographic impressions on sensitized plates."

"I've never been much of a fan of modern art. I guess I don't understand it."

"Don't tell my thesis professor, but neither do I." She swallowed hard. "Just another little joke." She cleared her throat. "Very little. Um. Let me guess — you like to know what you're looking at."

Good lord, was that a hint of a smile? "I guess so. Yes, that's true. A black square with blue lines around it looks like a black square with blue lines around it to me. Not art."

"How did the black square with blue lines around it make you feel?"

"Confused."

Teresa sipped her wine. "Maybe that's what the artist wanted — to make you confused about what art really is."

It *was* a smile, lordie lord. "Okay, I can buy that. Now explain fifty-seven of them."

"Everyone gets in a rut."

Ken actually grinned and Teresa did a mental happy dance. They could be one jolly family now. "I get it. You're joking again."

"I do that a lot. I'm my father's daughter."

"So am I."

Teresa pantomimed a wide-eyed peek over the table at Ken's lap. "Good disguise."

The smile disappeared. "I meant that I take after —"

"After your father." She managed to stop herself. "Sorry. I do that a lot, too. I come from a long line of people who finish other people's sentences."

"You can't blame genetics for everything."

Teresa blinked at him. "You're making a joke, aren't you?"

The man's face was utterly blank. "A very little one."

"You need an applause sign."

"You're not the first person to tell me that." He took the last bite of his cheesecake and watched his mother dancing. The expression on his face softened — there was a decent human being under there somewhere, Teresa thought.

But he doesn't like me, she added. What did that matter to her? Well, after tomorrow they were going to be related, sort of. This would not be the last time she had to spend time with him. It wasn't that he didn't like her, he didn't want to like her. She suspected why.

"What else did my father tell you about me?" She kept her smile disingenuous.

Ken lifted his eyebrows as if he hadn't thought about it. "That you have a Master's degree in art and you live in San Francisco."

"Actually, it's in fine arts administration. I can draw well, and my computer-assisted design is good, but I'm not the next Picasso." When Ken made no comment, she went on, "Did he tell you that my mouth often outpaces my brain?"

His lips twitched. "No, that he didn't mention, but I'm not surprised."

She gave him a narrow look. "Here's an example. I really should think better of this, but I'll just say it. Why don't you like me?"

He looked incredulous and guilty. "I barely know you."

"What you know, you don't like. Look, we're going to be family. I want my dad to be happy. You want your mom to be happy. If there's a problem I'd like to put it behind us so they don't get involved."

"There's nothing to discuss." He looked in vain at his dessert plate, but no distraction was available there.

"Just tell me. I think I can guess, anyway."

He gave her a long, level look. "I don't approve of the homosexual lifestyle."

Teresa nodded as she resisted the impulse stick him with her fork. "Well," she said slowly, "I don't approve of people who disapprove of millions of other people based solely on an assumption of how they live their lives. So we're even."

"I believe what my father taught me about the Bible."

"Funny, I believe what my father taught me about Christian love and tolerance." Their respective parents were headed for the table. Teresa said quickly, "We don't have to like each other. I'll be a pervert, you be a bigot and we'll just leave it at that."

"That's not what I meant," he hissed.

"Didn't you?" Teresa forced herself to smile as if she hadn't had such a pleasant conversation in ages. "Let's agree on one thing. Being honest." She added an inane giggle, then said to her father, "You guys look pretty good."

Melanie dropped into her chair and fanned herself with her napkin. "Your father is smooth."

"Smooth operator — oops! I wasn't supposed to say that."

Her father swatted her. "You are a troublemaker. Dance with your old man."

The slow swing rhythm was easy to follow. It was the first dance he'd ever taught her. Her father quickly asked the question she was dreading. "What do you think of Ken?"

She tried to be politic. "I'd never peg him for Melanie's son."

"He is a bit . . . dry."

"A-yup."

"A bit conservative."

"A-yup."

"I haven't had a chance to ask him his views on lesbians in the family, but I'm willing to guess he's a bit —"

"A-yup. You might have warned me."

"I thought I'd see if your undeniable charm won him over."

Teresa laughed. "I put my foot in it as usual."

"Mel tried to raise him properly, but Ken's father is a piece of work. It happens in the best of families."

"I'm just glad you're straight, Dad. She's the much better catch."

Her father pulled her close. "You know I love you, punkin."

"Yeah, I know."

Ken's voice in her ear startled her. "Mind if I cut in? It looks like both of our parents did a good job with dance lessons."

Teresa smiled brightly. "Lead me," she said breathily. As her father left the floor, Ken looked as if he regretted his impulse. "Just a little joke," she muttered.

"Not everything is a joke."

"It ought to be. Humor keeps the homicide rate down."

"I didn't come out here to argue." He turned her the same way her father had and she said nothing as she navigated a push-me-pull-you. When they were face to face again, he said, "I don't want you to think I'm a bigot."

"What would you call it?"

"I have a right to my opinion and it's based on my faith."

"That sounds a lot like what those two kids in Wyoming said. Good reasons to beat someone and leave him staked out on a fence post."

Ken's arms went rigid. "That was a terrible thing and indefensible. I would never condone it."

"Would you stop it?"

"Absolutely. You know, you're doing the same thing."

Teresa stopped dancing. "Let's look at the skyline, shall we?"

Ken nodded, and they stepped off the dance floor and through the doors that led to a small observation deck. "You think you understand me because I'm Christian."

"Not because you're Christian, but because you

pre-judged me." She turned her back to the silhouette of two pyramids and a Roman temple. "I get up every day. I go to work, do my laundry, scrub the sink. I pay my taxes. I go to the movies. To the library. Sometimes I go out with friends. I'm just hoping to meet someone who will make me happy. Who I can make happy."

"You can't deny that your lifestyle by definition means you're promiscuous."

Teresa shook with anger. "You're a charming fellow, you know that? How do you define *promiscuous*?" She was not promiscuous, and she didn't have to tell him that lack of opportunity was the reason.

"Sex outside marriage."

She gestured at the wide gold band he wore. "First of all, if gay people could get married a whole bunch of us wouldn't be having sex outside marriage. And so what if we do?" Her voice trembled on the last word.

"It's immoral." The turned-down mouth was in full evidence.

"You know what, Ken? I have to get up every day in a world where a man can stalk two women out hiking for several days, shoot them after he sees them kissing, and then claim that uncontrollable disgust made him do it. You have to get up in a world where most people are having more and better sex than you. I'm surprised you can get out of bed in the morning in the face of all that horror."

His jaw was mulish. "Sometimes it is hard to get up. Watching people every day squander the gift of life."

"Do you really think it's better for someone to live a lie, deceive their loved ones, pretend to be someone they're not? Is Christ really that cruel? And I have never understood the Book of Job."

"Don't tell my pastor, but neither have I."

Teresa's mouth dropped open. "Are you making a joke?"

"A very little one."

"But ... but," she spluttered. "I'm all worked up for a fight!" Her heart was racing, her palms sweating. She hadn't argued with anyone like this since ... never.

"My body clock is three hours ahead of yours. I'm all worked up for a long night's sleep."

"Has anything I've said made an impact?"

"I'm confused."

"Well, think of gay people like black boxes with blue lines around them."

His smile was tired. "Art?"

"Painted by God to keep you confused ... and flexible."

He let that go. "Has anything I said made an impression on you?"

Teresa's anger evaporated. "Well, not all so-called Christians are bloodthirsty members of a lynch mob." It was unfair that tolerance had to work both ways. Her father and his silly ideas of morality.

He leaned on the railing. "I'll admit I didn't want to find anything admirable about you. You're nothing like I thought you would be."

"See where preconceived notions can get you?" She felt very wise.

"Can we not have this conversation again?"

"I'm willing if you are. After all, we're getting married in the morning."

"Ding dong the bells are gonna chime."

She tucked her hand under his proffered arm, thinking that life at the turn of the century was pretty fucking weird.

The wedding itself was uneventful. Teresa found it all the sweeter for the spontaneity. She kept to herself her relief that the chapel did not have an Elvis impersonator — she knew her father's passion for all things Elvis.

As she and Ken were waiting for their parents to finish with the license, a giddy couple kissed their way from the door to the sign-in book.

"Is that how you spell your last name?" The man had his hand halfway up the woman's skirt.

Ken rolled his eyes. Out of the side of his mouth he muttered, "Six months."

Teresa sucked in her cheeks. "Is that the day they get divorced or the baby's due date?"

He chuckled. "Both, probably."

"Now think about it. Is that what was being protected by the Defense of Marriage Act?"

Ken's sigh was long-suffering. "I thought we had this conversation."

"Well, we didn't have *this* conversation. This is an all-new conversation."

Ken looked disapproving for about five seconds, then he laughed with a shrug. "Tell me this — are all gay women as charming as you are?"

"Well, I tell ya." Teresa looked at the ceiling. "Of the hundreds of thousands I've met I would have to say the answer is . . . no. Mostly because they show an appalling lack of judgment in not wanting to sleep with me." She abruptly thought of Rayann Germaine and the way she had felt in Teresa's arms. She goose-pimpled. "Do all Christians have as good a sense of humor as you do? You're laughing at all my jokes. This is great, 'cause you haven't heard them before. I can do my best stuff."

"You remind me of Ellen."

Teresa did her best to look offended. "I am wearing a nineteen-thirties vintage suit, pearl gray. The jacket and skirt side-button similar to what Katharine Hepburn wore in *Adam's Rib*."

"And your point is?"

"My point, and I do have one, is that Ellen would be wearing slacks." She was sure that most of the joke went right over his head, but he laughed anyway.

She decided she liked him sufficiently not to feel as if the family honor had been compromised by his inclusion. She would make it her personal goal for the cause to make Ken stop and think before he voted anti-gay. She'd be the little lesbian on his shoulder.

"So, married man and married lady, what now?" Teresa liked the way her father's smile had deepened. He was illuminated from the inside. "I mean if you two want to be alone Ken and I will find something to amuse us."

Melanie beamed. She gave her new husband a look that said, "They *are* getting along." She indicated the door. "Actually, we have a surprise for you. The limo should be outside."

The surprise was a sumptuous lunch and afternoon at a new resort that featured an indoor garden with over twenty thousand blooms. They wandered the grounds to see two dozen fountains and, to Teresa's vast interest, they toured the extensive art museum and gallery. The whole place reminded her of estates in France.

She was admiring a Hieronymous Bosch replica — it made her think of that woman yet again, which was not fair — when she heard Ken say, "Well, I'll be darned."

She turned. "What?"

"Look." He pointed.

"It's a chartreuse square with red lines around it."

"I looked and I thought — gay people come in all colors."

Teresa chortled. "You'd better be careful — Satan can quote art books for her purpose."

"Teresa, may I quote your father?"

"Yeah," she said warily.

"Shup."

She really was offended this time. "You don't know me well enough to tell me to shup."

Her father breezed by, saying, "Reese, everyone who has ever met you knows you well enough to want you to shut up."

"Oh! Years of filial devotion and this is what I get?" Teresa looked at Melanie for support. "For this I let him father me?"

Melanie sighed. "They're just men, Teresa."

"Melanie, you can call me Reese." Over her shoulder she said to Ken, "But you can't."

She let the colors of a Stuart Davis canvas claim her emotions, which were as jumbled as the painting — all red and gold and shocking orange. Always an only child, one parent for as long as she could remember, and now this family dynamic was happening. She hadn't really asked for it. She wasn't sure she'd missed much. Spending a year with her mother's mother in France had given her all the taste for high-strung matriarchs she ever wanted. So she would not think of Melanie as a mother, but she and Ken were now part of the family. It was disconcerting to her sense of the world. But her father was happier than she had ever seen him and that was worth an adjustment to reality on her part.

It occurred to her that if life got rough she wouldn't be able to run home to daddy because Mel would be there too. She knew she should be grateful to have Melanie's affection and support, but she hadn't realized that she was losing something in the bargain.

Crap, she thought. I really am going to have to grow up. You'll be twenty-eight very soon, she reminded herself. And you have a wrinkle. Crap.

6

"Tucker, you scared me to death!" Rayann bent to pick up the bag of treats she'd dropped. "And I brought emergency supplies just for you."

"Sorry, Ray." A fiendish Frankenstein face loomed over the bushes. Gory red goo bulged from one eye and sticky green stitches crisscrossed his forehead.

"Good makeup." The night was split by a piercing yowl and she jumped again. "Whose idea was this?"

"Joyce likes it." Tucker's grin proved that Joyce wasn't the only one. He dug into the treat bag she'd brought. "Cheese sticks, you're the best. Joyce won't let me eat any more of the stuff for the party."

Rayann could just imagine. Joyce reported it wasn't unusual for him, on the verge of sixteen, to absorb three peanut butter sandwiches after a full dinner and still look around for more. She pushed her way through the open front door and realized she had to navigate a maze to find the kitchen.

Where on earth did Joyce find black sheets? The maze forced her to stumble into two mummies and a sulfurous cadaver. Halfway through, Frankenstein jumped out at her again and did not look in the least sorry when she yelped.

Teddy appeared from the backyard, dragging his left leg behind him. "Welcome to Ghothly Manor," he lisped. He wore gray sweats and a hunter's cap with the flaps down. There was an enormous hump on his back.

"Did you get that moving all the furniture?"

He straightened. "Yes."

"You love it," Joyce informed him. She was fetchingly clad in a Catwoman costume, complete with tail, ears and stiletto heels.

"Wow, you look great," Rayann said, then worried she had put too much feeling into it. Joyce had long since proven her acceptance of lesbians and willingness to be friends, but sometimes she reacted awkwardly to certain types of comments.

She took Rayann's admiration in stride, however. "Thank you." She sent a pointed-dagger look at Teddy. "Some people notice."

"I worthip you, Mithreth. Igor think Joyth thwell." Teddy lurched toward her.

Joyce thrust a plate of appetizers at him. "Igor, take these outside."

"Igor obey." He slunk toward the patio.

"I feel totally outclassed," Rayann admitted. "I cheated with my costume." She tapped the name badge that adorned her suit jacket lapel. She'd dressed in all-black, but the nametag proclaiming her status as Union Representative for Witch's Local 1313 was her only costume.

"That's cute," Joyce said. "Very clever, and you didn't have to spend an hour letting out a costume seam. Come out to the patio."

Heat lamps kept the chilly night air at bay. From the patio she could glimpse parties on either side as well. *You'd like this, and Tucker is getting so tall.*

She said hello to Teddy's assistant and her husband. She'd met them at Louisa's memorial. The assistant wore a T-shirt that said "Middle-aged fat chick." Her husband's said "Chubby Hubby." It was a relief to see others who hadn't rented costumes.

Teddy offered the appetizers and Rayann managed to nibble. Everything tasted like cardboard to her. *I'd give anything for your ham and eggs, Lou. Or your apple pie.*

"Don't leave without talking to me, Ray." Teddy scratched under his cap. "I think we can finalize the lawsuit and get it over with."

"That would be great." She swallowed hard. "I decided yesterday to sell the bookstore to Ricki, and at the price she offered."

"Great. I think that's really wise. She loves the place as much as Mom did, and having lived upstairs since you and Mom moved, she knows what she's getting."

"Ricki's thrilled. I'm going to loan her the money, carry the paper myself. There's no point in her paying fees and stuff like that. Her willingness to work like a slave was the reason we could find a separate residence at last. It'll be hard enough to make ends meet." Meanwhile, the house she and Louisa had moved to was still in disrepair. She had no energy for anything. Coming to this party had taken a monumental effort of will.

"Don't I know it? I'll do the mortgage paperwork and the trust deed — it's really easy. You could do them yourself if you wanted."

"You do them — I can't think that hard." She was joking, but Teddy's expression said he believed her.

"How's the job front coming?" He sounded far too casual.

"Nothing exciting. Every once in a while, Tony still bugs me to come back, but it's not what I want anymore." *It's where I was when I lost you — I can't go back.*

"Are you doing any work? Woodwork, I mean."

She wanted to ask him why he was so interested. But she knew why. "I'm working on some small pieces for Christmas gifts. Thanks for telling me that Joyce likes calla lilies, by the way." She hadn't had time to handmake Christmas gifts in six years — since she'd gone back to advertising. She had all the time in the world now, but her chisels needed sharpening. Maybe next week she'd take them in.

More guests arrived and the doorbell rang incessantly. Tucker gravitated between the food and scaring trick-or-treaters. Rayann made conversation for a while, then drifted back into the house. She wandered into Teddy's home office and sat down to look at the picture of his mother he still kept on the credenza.

You looked great that day. It had been taken in Scotland. Louisa's black and silver hair was flying in the wind, streaming out over emerald green hills and the dark green ocean. She looked like a Druid priestess.

"I thought I'd find you in here." Teddy, sans hump, eased onto the sofa next to her.

"Sorry," she said quickly. "I don't know that many people."

"No problem. I'm glad you could make it. Joyce really knocks herself out."

"Joyce is great."

"I got lucky the second time around." Since Tucker's mother had never been in contact with ex-husband or son after leaving when Tucker was a baby, Rayann definitely agreed with him.

Teddy went on, "Anyway, I have the proposed settlement from the trucking company's insurance lawyers. They came up with the extra million, which means we'll have enough to buy that building for the Oakland Women's Center. Nancy already has two subtenants lined up for the first floor, a family-services lawyer and a security company owned by women."

Rayann felt a genuine flicker of interest. "That sounds great. A perfect match." *And you would have loved this, too.*

"The settlements for you and me and Tucker are the same and there's also enough to double what we thought for the other charities. If you invested wisely and lived simply you could do almost anything. Didn't you teach before you met Mom?"

"Way back when. It didn't suit me."

"Well, you could do almost anything."

"Lucky me." She had meant it as a joke, but her voice broke.

After an uncomfortable silence, he said, "I sometimes have the oddest urge to pick up the phone and call her. I haven't forgotten she's not there, and yet I still get the urge."

"I know what you mean," Rayann said. She knew all too well.

He picked up Louisa's picture. "Why is it you have to be pushing forty before you appreciate that time is too short? I spent all those years being a jerk about her being gay. What a waste."

Tears rose but she forced them down. She had made it nearly three months without crying. She was not going to start now.

"When Chris died, I missed her so much. She was the only other parent I'd ever known. I knew how Mom was feeling. But I pretended I didn't really care. I said it wasn't as if she was family." He let the words out as if he'd held them in too long, and not saying them now was more than he could bear. "She had lost the love of her life and I made her pretend she was just a friend because I didn't want anyone to know my mom was a lesbian. She went through it alone because I made a scene every time Danny came to visit. All the nights she must have spent crying it out so I wouldn't see. What a selfish bastard." He scrubbed his sleeve over his eyes.

"Teddy, she loved you."

"It wasn't until you came along that I let her be a person. I told her I was sorry about the way I reacted to you. But I never could say how sorry I was about Chris."

"She knew. She had to know. She understood you better than you understood yourself."

He put the photograph down, then looked at her with compassion. The resemblance of his eyes to his mother's was too painful to endure. She studied her thumbs. "Poor Ray. Comforting me when you're still getting over it yourself."

There was no "getting over it." Rayann didn't understand how anyone could think she would get over it.

"And I didn't mean — when I said that Chris was the love of her life — I didn't mean you weren't."

"I know. She once said she didn't know what she'd done to get lucky twice." She had made her peace with Chris's existence a long time ago. Part of Chris had been in Louisa, and she had loved all of Louisa.

There was a sudden burst of music from the living room. "Tucker's started up *The Rocky Horror Picture Show*, I see."

She did the "Time Warp" with Tucker — she'd taught him the steps, after all — then left shortly thereafter. Between double-parked cars and wandering costumed ghouls and goblins, traffic was horrible.

She had an urge to go to the Castro, but the thought of the crowd made her decide against it. What would she do if she went, anyway? Go to a bar? Look for that woman again?

Everyone said that time heals all wounds. Everyone said she needed to get on with her life. Everyone, particularly Judy, said she should go to a grief counselor.

Everyone could go to hell, she thought. None of

them had lost Louisa's love. She viciously cut off another driver on the approach to the bridge.

The rush of anger left her shaking, then exhausted. She'd been fighting it for weeks. She didn't want to be angry. She wanted to be in control. Numb. Which meant another night at home. It wasn't too early in the season to watch *Miracle on 34th Street*. Louisa had loved it.

"How are you coming along with those?" Carla leaned over the banister from the floor above.

"Great. This is a perfect project to take up on a slow day." Teresa had set about sorting the canvases as soon as she'd arrived.

"I'm sure everyone is at the day-after sales. Did you have a good Turkey Day?"

"I'm still stuffed. My roommate wanted to impress her new girlfriend with her culinary prowess, and I was a lucky bystander." Teresa indicated the stacks of small canvases around her. "I've got the wheat sorted from the chaff. And this one," she said as she picked up a canvas and held it under the desk lamp, "is undoubtedly the best of the lot. It will have to be authenticated, but I'm pretty sure it's a Klee sketch."

"A Klee?" Carla's head disappeared and her heels rapped along the floor and down the staircase toward Teresa. "You're kidding!"

Teresa wasn't perturbed by Carla's patent disbelief. An estate gift of 100 mixed canvases, most of little value, would not be where she'd go looking for a Paul

Klee, sketch or painting. But she was reasonably sure she knew a Klee when she saw one. Chalk one up for art school. "It could be an imitation, I suppose. But I recognize the final piece this sketch was a preliminary for."

Carla took the frame in her hands as if it was made of eggshell. "Did you hold it up to the light?"

"Um, no." It hadn't occurred to her.

Carla turned the frame over. "It looks like it was specially framed so that the back could be viewed, too."

"I thought that might be to see the date." She pointed at the small inscription.

"There could be more to it than that, if I know anything at all about Klee. Let's go look in a bright light."

They went to the small balcony off the second floor. Carla held the small frame up so that sunlight streamed through it. "Ah! There it is! His watermark!"

With the sunlight illuminating every grain and weave in the paper, Teresa could see the artist's signature watermarked in the paper. "I'd never have looked for that. I didn't know to look."

"Experience, my dear, it's all in the experience."

"Do you think the family knew it was in here?"

"I doubt it — it would be worth thousands . . . Look at the condition, though. At one time, someone knew what it was." She handed it back. "Go find the history of it, girlfriend. Good eye!"

Her heart pounding with jubilation, Teresa sat down at the terminal that would let her sign on to the Network for the Fine Arts. She confined herself to humming. The hours were long, the tasks sometimes mind-numbing, but she'd certainly won Carla's respect and the respect of the board members for whom she'd done special projects.

A Paul Klee, she congratulated herself. In amongst dime-a-dozen watercolors and reproductions, she'd found a valuable piece of art. She had always liked Klee's clean lines and wire art.

According to the NFA, the final piece was held by the Boston Museum of Fine Arts. She wondered what they might like to trade as a more or less permanent loan if Carla wanted to loan them the sketch to go with the final piece.

She also found that there were believed to be at least two dozen sketches, but only seven were accounted for in the NFA. All were held by private collectors with appraisal dates. It looked better and better that what she'd found was genuine and previously unlisted.

She bounced into Carla's office. "I'm almost certain that it's genuine. I've got an e-mail in to Boston, they've got the final —" Carla looked as if she was going to cry. "What's wrong?"

"Paul Sallter died this morning."

"Whoa." Teresa sat down. Paul Sallter underwrote a quarter of their operating budget. "I didn't know he was sick."

"He wasn't. Heart attack. I'm a terrible person," Carla added.

"Why?"

"I liked Paul and all I can think about is, what are we going to do? I'm pretty sure the current Mrs.

Sallter will have lots of other plans for the Sallter fortune." She snorted. "The new Mrs. Sallter prefers wearable art."

"He'll have left something in his will," Teresa said with far more conviction than she felt.

"I just hope we're not all looking for work next month. We didn't get this month's check yet, either." A tear ran down her cheek. "It seems so petty to worry about it right now. He was a nice person."

"I'm sure everything will be fine," Teresa said. She'd never met Mr. Sallter, so she didn't feel in the least bit restrained from petty worries like if she was going to get her next paycheck. Carla was really pale. If she was worried about her job, then where did Teresa stand?

Then it hit her. At the bottom of the totem pole, that's where. All of the other assistants had way more tenure than she did.

Vivian was not a lot of help when Teresa unburdened herself that night. "No one thinks they have a job forever anymore."

"But I really like it. And I finally finished the new database and we got all the pieces security-tagged. I was going to get to do some fun stuff finally."

Vivian brushed lint off her black suede high heels. "Well, you should start looking right now, just in case. By the time you've had some interviews, you'll know if you need to take another position."

It was good advice. She hated the thought of looking, though. "I'll never find anything in museum work. I'll have to look for computer design. And that means going back to advertising, most likely."

"It pays well. Until something better comes along."

Vivian strapped on the shoes, then smoothed her red sheath. She had another date with Kim, which meant Teresa most likely had the place to herself for the night. They usually went to Kim's place, two or three nights a week since Kim's roommate worked nights. Imagining all the fun Vivian was going to have did not improve her spirits.

She slumped on the sofa. "Well, you can bet I'm avoiding the place where I worked before like the plague. There must be someplace decent to work, where you're not just a cog in a machine."

"You dreamer, you. See you tomorrow night," Vivian said over her shoulder.

Teresa dug out the job classifieds part of the *Chronicle,* and stretched out in front of the TV. She found nothing to her liking in the paper, not one thing she'd send a résumé to.

Discouraged, she flipped channels. Violent, violent, inane, way too heterosexual, inane, inane — wait, that one was a Bond flick. The perfect combination of violence, inanity and heterosexuality for her tastes. She woke up after midnight and muddled herself into bed. At one, she was awakened by amorous noises from Vivian's room. For whatever reason they'd come back here — oh joy.

Just when she thought her life was going along a track she liked, she was totally derailed. And her roommate had found a steady girlfriend when her own long hours had kept her from pursuing romance. Something was just not fair about turning twenty-eight.

"Oh yeah, oh yeah," was being chanted on the other side of the wall.

She rolled over and put her head under a pillow. It did not muffle the sound of the headboard thumping into the wall.

She sang "American Pie" fairly loudly, trying to remember all the words. All she could think was that everyone seemed to be having more sex than she was, and better sex at that. She was beginning to understand why Ken resented it. She couldn't remember the last time she'd had sex with another person in the room — almost, in an alley with that woman didn't count.

"Do it!"

She sang louder. "Do it to me one more time..." Gak.

The ohs and yesses were running into each other. It sounded like Vivian was enjoying giving orders and Kim was obliging. She plugged her ears with her fingers and chanted, "I'm not listening, I'm not listening," until the thumping stopped.

She unplugged her ears and waited cautiously. Sighing, cooing. Thank God they were done.

She was almost asleep again when the "Oh baby, oh baby," began. She vowed that tomorrow night, no matter what, she would get out of the house and go someplace where single women could be found.

"Harder!"

Even if it was that men's bar where she'd almost seduced that woman. Right now she really wished she had. She shuddered as she remembered the cold brick against her back.

"Don't stop!"

The feel of her soft skin, those full breasts.

"All night, baby, all night!"

She stumbled out of bed, jammed *Die Hard III* into the VCR and turned it up loud.

Ken was right. Sex outside marriage was evil. Especially when it was possible to hear, over the sound of three exploding armored cars, "God you're incredible oh God more oh harder God me oh God I'm oh God . . ."

"Mom, I can't face any more turkey. You're on your own with the leftovers." Rayann twined the phone cord around her finger. "I ate three dinners yesterday."

"Good, you've lost too much weight."

She let that slide. "You like apples and walnuts in your stuffing. Joyce likes celery and mushrooms. Marilyn made it Danny's favorite way — cornbread and chestnuts." Just thinking about all the food she'd consumed was making her queasy again.

"I forgot to tell you yesterday that I've heard rumors about a shake-up at Liman's. Do you want me to keep you posted?"

Automatically, Rayann answered, "Sure." If she had any intention of working anywhere in advertising, Liman's was a place that would suit her. It was not as if she was busy with anything else. The only reason she'd even picked up a chisel in her workshop was to make a few Christmas presents. It had hardly been a creative impulse. "A shake-up there? That's unusual."

"I think someone is retiring, actually, so they're going to reorganize a little. That's about as dramatic as it gets at Liman's. So are you going to do any shopping? The sales are supposed to be good this year."

"In that mess? I've gotten addicted to uncrowded shopping conditions, I'm afraid."

"But braving the crowds is part of the fun."

"You always were crazy that way."

"Oh well," her mother sighed. "I guess I'll have to go alone."

Rayann settled into the comfy chair again and opened *Mrs. Dalloway*. It was Louisa's favorite Virginia Woolf.

The phone rang.

It was the third call that morning. She let the machine pick it up. Judy wanted to know if she was up to shopping with a fat lady. Her fingers tightened around the book. She'd accepted three invitations for Thanksgiving get-togethers because she hadn't really been out since Halloween. Yesterday she'd turned down three more offers for outings. Joyce had wanted to go shopping. Jim had invited her for a round of golf on Saturday. Teddy had wanted her to come over for the Forty-niners game on Sunday.

Why can't they just leave me alone?

Louisa didn't answer. She hadn't been answering since the settlement check from the trucking company had arrived.

She clenched her jaw, trying to work past the sudden rage. Her scalp broke out in a sweat and her nails left vivid half-moons in her palms. The anger subsided finally, but every day it was more difficult to work through it.

Unable to sit still, she went for a walk. Their new house was on the fringe of a little enclave not far from Lake Merritt. They'd been lucky to find a house big enough to provide extra rooms for a home office they could both use and a sunny den Rayann had set up as a workshop. It wasn't a particularly trendy neighborhood, being too close to downtown Oakland for some people's tastes, but the location couldn't have been more convenient for them. It was only six blocks to the bookstore and only a little farther to a rapid transit station. When the weather was bad Rayann took a cab — Louisa had always walked, rain or shine. At least she had for the short time she had been walking to work instead of simply going downstairs.

As Rayann turned the corner she left behind the echoes of the empty house and the shadows of plans that would never be completed. Her feet found the familiar path to the bookstore without any particular thought on her part. As she walked up the street she relived her first walk to its door.

The Common Reader hadn't changed much. Like all of the buildings in the area, it sat above the street on a raised foundation, as if in danger of flooding. The bookstore occupied the bottom floor. Through the second-story windows she could glimpse Venetian blinds. She knew what lay beyond them like she knew her own body — the living room and kitchen divided by a bar-height counter, the bedroom that had been hers until she'd given it up for Louisa's. The memory of the bookstore and their apartment above it was more poignant and painful than the new house.

From the sidewalk she could see Ricki's "This weekend only" sale signs just under the store name. She hadn't been able to find the strength to go inside, so all the negotiating with Ricki had been done by phone or at a local café over coffee. If she went inside, it would be for the first time since the accident. Not today, she thought. *I can't do it today.*

A customer with an armload of books came down the stairs. She heard Ricki's voice, then Ricki was at the door, looking down to the street. "I'll give you a call when it's in — Rayann!"

She had to go in now. "I was just out for a walk," she said as she climbed the stairs. Ricki gave her a hug and pulled her inside.

The smell washed over her. The smell of old books . . . it smelled like Louisa's hands and her hair.

"I just wanted to thank you again," Ricki was saying. "I feel like the luckiest woman on the face of the planet. I've found the perfect person to be part-time — she might want to buy in, too. Isn't that great?"

"Good for you." Ricki hadn't changed anything except the front displays. It was so easy to believe that Louisa was just out of sight in the side room they'd called "The Women's Reader." Or she was up-stairs making lunch. In just a moment Rayann would hear the throaty laugh and the quick tread of Louisa's feet on the stairs.

She recognized some of the customers as regulars. The small talk was not as bad as she thought it'd be. No one brought up Louisa and she didn't have to lie that she was getting on with her life.

Being there was too much, though. The smell, the way the floor creaked, the buzz of the cash register, it was all too much. She had fallen head over heels in love with Louisa, surprising her twenty-nine-year-old sensibilities with an aching physical need for a woman twenty-seven years her senior — a year older than her own mother. She'd denied how she felt, then admitted and mightily struggled to keep her secret from Louisa. And all the while those sounds and the aroma of literature and the passion of poetry had been in the background. In a way, she'd been seduced by the bookstore first. She could not go to the back of the store where they'd once made love, all in a rush, like teenagers too eager to find someplace more private. The apartment upstairs where they'd spent nearly nine years together was full of memories too vivid to be endured. She was glad she would never have to come back here again.

She bought a new book on the history of the gay civil rights movement, then left as soon as she could, never once looking into the side room, pretending that Louisa was in there, that everything was like it once had been.

She was getting tired, but she forced herself up the block to the retirement residence. It was the only regular commitment she was keeping these days, and she hadn't visited in several weeks. The book was for Hazel Schoernsson, who might be completely deaf but whose eyesight was as good as ever.

As always, she thought the little apartment seemed smaller without Greta's gentle presence. Her death from rapidly spreading liver cancer had happened two years ago. She'd wasted away almost overnight, it had seemed, certainly more quickly than Louisa had. As it had been happening, Rayann had thought that someday she might be watching Louisa through a similar death. She'd been prepared for an illness, maybe cancer. Something like that. Not being thrown twenty-four feet by a truck.

The urge — all too familiar — to find the driver

and strangle him with her bare hands made her fingers curl and blood pound in her temples. She sometimes pictured him being forced to drink beer after beer after beer until it killed him. Prison was too good for him.

Money was no revenge. The settlement check sat in the bank. She had no plans for spending a dime.

Hazel was too stubborn to let Rayann make the tea, and Rayann could tell that today was a bad hip day.

They sipped the tea while Hazel admired the book, sometimes talking so quietly Rayann could hardly hear her. There was nothing wrong with Hazel's mind or her self-discipline. The visiting nurse assured Rayann that Hazel never missed a meal and was always doing light exercise when her hips would let her. But it was clear to Rayann that Hazel was living in a world where Greta still shared every thought and every care, just as they had for nearly sixty years. They'd run away together on the eve of Greta's wedding, immigrated and passed themselves off as sisters, never telling anyone they were lovers until Rayann had started working in Louisa's bookstore. Now a small rainbow flag was pinned next to the apartment's front door, in the space permitted for "expressions of personal identity."

Their conversation was mostly pointing and smiles with Rayann scrawling comments on a small white board. Hazel brought out her most recent collection of newspaper clippings she thought Rayann would be interested in. It was just about the only news Rayann took in these days. Louisa had been a demon for keeping up on current events.

Just another way I've let you down.

So little about Hazel reminded her of Louisa that she stayed until it was nearly sunset. Hazel shooed her out with dire predictions about the weather and winter colds. Rayann fondly kissed her good-bye — her fussing sounded just like Greta.

It wasn't far from there to Lake Merritt. A sharp-edged wind raised tiny whitecaps across the surface. She avoided the northern part of the lake and traipsed instead the long way through Laney College to get to a hole-in-the-wall Korean diner serving the spicy noodles that had been one of Louisa's favorite dishes. The red pepper kept her warm inside during the cold walk home.

She was exhausted and yet she couldn't sit still. She'd planned on watching *Howard's End*, one of Louisa's more recent favorites, but for once she found the pace slow, the dialogue stilted. Even Emma Thompson didn't intrigue her, and usually Rayann could not look away from any scene with Emma in it.

Her lack of concentration frustrated her. She paced the house, stepping over the rolls of wallpaper and around the ladder by habit. Her shirt itched.

She dug in the hamper for something sort of clean and less itchy. On her way back to the living room she stubbed her toe on the ladder. The ladder toppled into a side table and one of Louisa's pictures tipped onto the floor.

She picked it up — the glass had cracked across Louisa's face.

What, is this some kind of fucking metaphor? Blinded by a lightning bolt of rage, Rayann threw the frame as hard as she could and ignored the sound of breaking glass. She yanked the table over. More frames shattered on the tile floor. She heaved the ladder into the hallway and tripped over the table, landing heavily on the rubble on the floor. Her left hand came up bloody from glass, but she paid no attention as she stumbled into the kitchen.

It was as if someone else was in the house. Someone else picked up the half-empty bottle of gin and threw it against the refrigerator. Someone else was screaming. Someone else stumbled into the so-called workroom and picked up the magnifying glass.

"This is all shit!" The glass flew into the hall. She snatched up her chisels and one by one threw them knife-fashion into the hall, too. The largest was in her hand and she turned on the piece she'd been trying to start.

It was supposed to be an homage to love, a memory of passion. She'd told herself once it was done she could find a job, move forward. But she hadn't even finished the sketches.

"This is shit, too," she said grimly. With ferocious determination she brought the chisel down on the top of the block. That it hardly dented the ironwood only made her more angry and determined.

She'd had the block for years. She'd moved it into Louisa's apartment over the bookstore, then into this house. No more. It was a millstone around her neck. It represented all her failures as an artist, as a person, as a lover.

She picked up the hammer, seated the chisel into a nearly invisible ripple in the wood and struck hammer to chisel with all her might.

The chisel handle shattered under the blow and the blade underneath sliced into her palm. In a moment of stillness, Rayann thought, "How could I be so stupid?" Then the sight of blood spilling across the surface of the wood made her run to the bathroom. The cut was deep and long, and the bleeding wouldn't stop.

It wasn't easy getting to the emergency room by herself, but she was so embarrassed at what had happened that she couldn't bear to have anyone see her, or the house. By the time she saw a doctor the bleeding had stopped but she was shaking inside. Seven stitches was nothing compared to how badly she could have hurt herself. She had completely lost control. She didn't know how to stop it from happening again.

It was after midnight when she walked into the house again, her right hand throbbing under a tightly wrapped bandage. The reek of gin slapped her, and although she was exhausted, she made herself clean up the mess. It took much longer with just one hand. She wasn't angry anymore, just so tired. The painkillers left her feeling disconnected. She didn't mind.

7

Teresa surveyed herself in Vivian's long mirror and buttoned the last button on the cuffs of the vintage jacket. All the feasting at her dad's over Christmas had made the waist a little more snug. If the rain let up she would go for a run later.

It had not been raining in L.A. The sky had even been what passed for blue in Southern California. She would have stayed longer and soaked up the rays, but instead she was pounding the pavement in hopes of landing gainful employment before she had to borrow money from her dad to make the rent. Working for a curator's salary hadn't left her any savings, and two weeks' notice hadn't been enough to find a job before she was without a paycheck.

She missed the museum a lot. She missed the quiet hum of visitors and she missed her coworkers. Carla had been a good boss. She'd learned a lot from her, not just about running a museum, but also working with employees, peers, clients. Five months' watching and learning had not been enough and her abrupt termination, along with two other assistants, would be painful for a while.

She smoothed the jacket. She was presentable enough. She glared at the wrinkle on her temple and the one that forked from it. Don't obsess, she warned herself. She had a date for New Year's Eve, a woman named Susan she'd met at the Lace Place. She didn't know if it would lead anywhere, but at long last she had a date. The vintage suit had certainly been worth every penny.

She looked businesslike enough for the financial district but not cookie cutter. The ad agency she was interviewing at was definitely a free-thinking group, but she wanted to be taken seriously. Her computer design skills were respectable and she didn't want anyone thinking she could be treated like a lightweight. She was not going to repeat the past.

Her first misgivings occurred as she waited in the reception area. She counted seven pairs of Birkenstocks, four patchwork vests and three tie-dyed shirts. A huge print of a Grateful Dead album cover adorned the waiting area. There was an assortment of the expected deathly pale, black-clad artiste types and all of them looked at her askance. Compared to them, she looked like an investment banker.

She unbuttoned her jacket and undid the collar of her shirt. The scarf disappeared into her purse.

She was a little nervous about the interview. She had sent in her résumé and gone through a phone interview with a person from the human resources department. Now she was waiting for the CEO, who apparently liked to interview all the applicants personally. The H.R. person had said the turnover of the seventy or so employees was so low that it didn't take much of his time. Maybe I should be nervous, she thought. There must be tons of people hankering for any job at such a steady and well-regarded local firm.

Someone had dubbed Liman's the Ben & Jerry's of advertising. The firm took no business that offended CEO and Founder Philip Liman's political sensibilities — including liquor and tobacco — and their work was high quality. When she'd read up on Liman's, she'd found they were generally regarded as quacks when it came to running a business, and geniuses when it came to advertising.

She had really liked everything she read and she was eager to get this job. It was the best "fit," as career advisors called it, of the six interviews she had lined up, but she had to make sure that she wasn't going to be working for some egomaniac.

Philip Liman was affable enough when she was finally shown into his office. "Are you sure that advertising is the right field of work for you?"

His first question caught her off guard. "I don't know for sure." Wrong answer, she thought. "I want to feel as if my skills are being used well, that I can participate in a creative process. I don't want to sell my soul to do it, or be somebody's hamster on a twenty-four-hour-a-day wheel." She stopped blabbering and found a nervous smile. "I'm still young. I still think these things are possible." There. She'd put all her desires on the table.

"Let's look at your portfolio."

She'd arranged it carefully. She had nothing to show from the first job, so it was all undergrad and graduate work. She'd done posters for the campus Race for Life, several America Night event posters when she'd been at the Sorbonne, and an entire P.R. package — logo to letterhead — for a family planning clinic. In between the commercial art displays, she'd sprinkled her freehand drawings in colored pencil to demonstrate her range and ability at composition.

As he turned the pages, he said, "Your year abroad is what intrigued me the most. We have so many locally trained people that we felt we could use a breath of fresh air. Tell me about it."

Teresa remembered to breathe so her voice wouldn't quaver. "My grandmother lives in Paris and without her willingness to provide room and board I would have probably stayed in the States. She wasn't an easy person to live with, but it was well worth the conflict." He's not interested in the personal stuff, she reminded herself. "The students and instructors were international, so the exposure I got was really broadening. I haven't had a chance to put it to practical use." She sounded like a school brochure.

"You would get lots of that here. What do you think you learned there that you wouldn't have learned at an American university?"

Images of Paris streets, French food, the sight of her first DaVinci, and musty classrooms mixed in her head with her unrelenting homesickness and her grandmother's volatile personality. It had been a year of extremes. "Oddly enough, I think I learned more about American masters there. I certainly saw a lot more art in Paris and on short field trips than I would have at home. There was also a valuable personal lesson." He didn't look bored, so she went on. "I know that my work is good. I knew that when I went. But graduate school including that year in Paris brought me into contact with people who have been honing and thinking about their life's creative effort since they were two."

He smiled. "I think I know what you mean."

"I just don't burn with that kind of fire. I really missed home, by that I mean the States. And once I grappled with the reality of the status of artists in this country — which is not great — I decided that a career in the arts didn't have to be as a practicing artist. That's why I changed my masters program to Fine Arts Administration."

"That brings us back to my first question — is a career in advertising what you're looking for?"

Well, there it was. Wrong answer, no job. But she couldn't lie. "Certainly not the typical career. Like I said, I want to feel like a contributing part of a team and not someone's lackey in the endless pursuit of money."

He turned over another page, saying, "I can certainly understand that." He stopped short and studied one of Teresa's favorite pieces. Layers of paper with two scalloped cutouts, each saturated in increasingly brilliant orange, led down to a smudged watercolor of tan, blue and yellow. He smiled. "It's like opening your eyes when you've been lying in the sun. Very creative."

"Thank you."

118

"I like what I see," he said. "There are times when we sorely need someone who is grounded in the basics of design. Our art department is full of self-taught smarties who get a little too wild from time to time. I'm a self-taught smartie, too. Half the time I don't know why what we do works."

Teresa didn't believe that for a second. "Well, I can say that I may have gone to art school, but a lot of people feel that art is not something you can really learn in a school."

"And advertising is not high art. It just uses some of the same skills."

She grinned. "This interview is not going the way I thought it would."

"I believe that the word most often used to describe this firm is 'unconventional.' You'll need to get used to that."

"Does that mean . . ." She gulped. "You mean I got the job?"

"Not quite. I misspoke — you do have my vote. You seem like the kind of artist that would really add to our skill set. Your next hurdle is an interview with Amy Bledsoe, the art director. She's a bit of a lame duck, having resigned for personal reasons, and it will take a while to find the right replacement. She wants to leave a fully staffed department in the interim. She'll also do a pretty hard-nosed job of explaining our philosophy."

"Ninety percent of the people who work at Liman's do it because this is a fabulous place to work." Amy Bledsoe was endlessly in motion. It was motion with purpose, not like Carla's anxious hovering for fear of taking two seconds too long to get where she needed to be. Most of their interview had been spent walking the art department floor. Teresa would wait patiently while Amy quickly reviewed or settled some matter, then went to the next cluster of cubicles.

All of the conversations were friendly, the atmosphere as collegial as any she could have hoped for. It was too good to be true. She pushed away the little voice that reminded her that just when she got settled and happy the other shoe would drop. For the life of her, though, she couldn't find any fault with the place or the people.

Amy was in motion again. "The other ten percent work here because they're crazy. And no matter what, if you don't fit in, it becomes pretty obvious pretty fast. We have a couple of rules. They're easy to follow. One. When you're here you pull your own weight. Two. You can make a good living working here, but you're not going to get rich. So stop trying. Three. When you have to, you're here twenty-four hours a day. Four. When you don't have to, you're not here at all."

"That seems pretty straightforward." Teresa stutter-stepped around a pile of videotapes. She had to lean forward to hear Amy over the blast of a soft drink jingle from a conference room.

"When you're on a project team you are expected to speak your mind. Going along with the crowd is not acceptable." Amy stopped abruptly and leaned into a cubicle. "Where's Wallace?" The response was muffled, then Amy said, "I'm going to have to deal with it. I can't let it go any longer."

Finally it appeared they were at Amy's office. It was large but cluttered with art boards, televisions with multiple VCRs, a sophisticated stereo system and a basketball hoop.

Amy followed Teresa's line of sight. "It relaxes me. Well, now I have two openings to fill. My last word of warning. We believe strongly in live and let live, but if your private habits prevent you from pulling your own weight, you're out. We function as a team because each and every person is here to do their part." Without pause, Amy went on, "So, when do you want to start?"

Teresa blinked, then found her voice. "I can start anytime. My curator's job ended on Christmas Eve."

Amy leafed through two stacks of paper on her desk, then yanked one out. "That sucks. Merry Christmas, you're fired." She leaned out her office door. "Henry! Where's Hen —"

A breathless young man rushed up.

"There you are. Give this to Leila or Doug. Thanks. I need a cup of coffee really bad." She glanced at Teresa. "Do you want anything?"

"No, I'm fine. Really," Teresa said.

The young man turned a friendly but slightly vacant smile on her. "I make good coffee. Everyone says so."

"I won't be here long enough to enjoy it," Teresa said. Her stomach rumbled. Her next stop was dinner.

He shrugged and hurried away with the papers.

"He makes fabulous coffee, like an angel," Amy said. "It's all that keeps me going sometimes."

"I look forward to having some."

"Did Philip tell you I'm leaving? Health reasons I won't go into. But the work will always be there."

"I'm sorry I won't get the chance to work with you," Teresa said. "But I'm very excited about this."

"Let's go see Diego." Amy was out the office door again, turning left and right through the cubicle groups. "Diego will be your senior for the first three months. He'll dump all the menial stuff he can on you, but that's how you learn." She rapped her knuckles on a cubicle frame. "Diego, I found the person you've been dying to train."

There was a groan, and Amy stood back to let Teresa into the cubicle. It was oversized compared to all the others, but when she saw Diego's wheelchair she understood. She took the two steps necessary into the cubicle to keep him from having to shift his chair and held out her hand. "Teresa Mandrell."

"You sing?" Diego had extraordinary eyes. They were a depthless black and overloaded with charm and suggestive warmth. Bedroom eyes, big time. His handshake was firm but not overwhelming.

"No relation. I don't even like country music."

"Blasphemer!" Diego flicked his gaze to Amy. "How could you do this to me?"

"Bye bye," Amy was saying. "You'll work it out." Henry appeared out of nowhere with a mug of coffee and a file folder for Amy. "Henry, I love you." They disappeared in the direction of Amy's office.

Diego waved his hand at a stack of folders and storyboards. "So when can I give you this pile of suicide-inducing minutiae?"

"Well, I can start anytime." She grinned ear-to-ear. "I can't believe I got the job."

"Why? You lie about something on your résumé?"

"No, it just feels really lucky."

"Please. If you weren't the right person you'd have never made it past Philip the benevolent dictator."

"If you say so. It's nice to be appreciated. Is everyone always in this good a mood?"

"This is the lull between Christmas and New Year's. Half the staff is on vacation."

"Oh. So it gets a little more noisy then, I guess."

Diego sighed. "Why do they always give me the lambs to slaughter?"

Teresa blinked. "Say again?"

He spread his hands in a gesture of helplessness. "It's always this quiet. Everyone here is always in a good mood. We love each other. No one ever yells. There's no stress and you'll just adore every minute of every day. So much so you won't mind sleeping here."

Teresa swallowed. That sounded more like the art department she had expected. " 'Kay. I can deal with all that."

"I will personally feed those words to you. I'll bet Amy didn't tell you about our commitment to punctuality."

"No, she didn't." What the heck was that?

"Don't be late to meetings. They start on time so they can end on time. Everyone who is late pays a buck a minute into the fund for the charity of the month. The max is ten bucks, plus you get volunteered to do shitwork." His gaze flicked to his screen as it announced he had mail. "It looks all easy-peasy on the outside, but underneath, this place is as much a machine as anywhere else. You just won't be slaving like a dog so some guy can have a vacation house in the Hamptons. Plus, you won't have to dig down for your best artistic impulses to sell a cigarette to a twelve-year-old."

"Those are big compensations. I'm not afraid of hard work."

"Ooh, doggie. And I get you for three months. This is so cool." His phone buzzed. "Go see Angela in H.R. to do all that salary and insurance stuff. That's back on Philip's floor — just ask reception. Do you really want to start this week? Take the rest of the year off, you'll need the stamina later."

Teresa chuckled. "Maybe that would be for the best. So I'll see you next week."

His voice followed her over the cubicles. "Staff meeting is at nine-fifteen pronto Monday morning. New person brings the muffins. We need at least a dozen big ones."

After she'd filled out the numerous forms and floated out of the building, her first order of business was dinner. She congratulated herself for landing on her feet. It had been terrific luck and maybe, she allowed, just a little bit of talent. She gobbled a sandwich and then, given that her paycheck would shortly be 25 percent larger, she let her credit card have its way with her at Georgiou's. New job meant new clothes. A royal purple blouse with an emerald suede collar had been calling her name.

"Thanks again for doing this, Ray." Judy waddled out of the elevator. "I'm glad you're backing us up."

"I have all the time in the world and Dee has the

schedule from hell. Really, it's no bother." The only thing that punctuated her weeks now was Judy's childbirth classes. She was Dedric's backup, and she went along whether Dedric could be there or not. Today Dedric didn't end her shift until after the class.

Rayann had not thought it possible to do less than she had before but she'd found a way. It was all she could do to lift her head from the pillow when she woke from one of her rare sleeps. She'd showered that morning for the first time in days and even managed a load of laundry. She'd have to do the same this Sunday when Nancy was holding a New Year's Day grand opening for the new Louisa May Thatcher Women's Center. She'd told Nancy that Louisa wouldn't have expected to have it named after her, but Nancy had insisted.

Judy pulled her capacious maternity dress hard against her enormous stomach. "I want them to take it out now."

"It's three weeks to your due date. From what I've heard, first babies are always late and the worst is yet to come." Who would have thought it was almost a brand new year and Judy's baby was almost here? The holiday season used to be a cycle of parties and celebrations. Louisa had loved the solstice concert at Davies Hall. She had spent Christmas with her mother and Jim, but otherwise December was a blur of nothing.

"You're such a ray of sunshine. No pun intended. God, my back is killing me."

"My godchild just wants to be taken seriously."

Judy rubbed her stomach fondly, then resumed her slow pace toward the parking garage. Her long coat, which was designed for Judy's regular stomach, flapped in the wind. "Oh, I take this baby very seriously. Kicks me all night and just for fun dances on my bladder every five minutes. Which makes fifty-minute therapy sessions hard to sit through."

"You always had a bladder the size of a pea."

"Put a bowling ball on your bladder and see how long you can hold it."

"And they say pregnancy makes a woman glow with happiness."

" 'They' are all men."

Rayann helped Judy lower herself into the passenger seat. The baby was going to get bigger before Judy pushed it out, which boggled Rayann's mind. Today's birthing class had emphasized the chemical reactions that made the cervix dilate, the birth canal more elastic, and how the baby's skull was in pieces to compress in the birth canal. But to Rayann it still seemed like pushing a basketball out a nostril. She admired Judy vastly for wanting to go through with it. She had no desire to do it herself.

Judy catnapped on the ride home. She fell asleep everywhere, she complained. Dedric was just parking in their driveway when Rayann pulled up. She had a familiar thrill at the sight of Dee in her navy blue uniform and gun belt with her night stick under one arm. She shook Judy. "Dee's home."

Judy snored.

"Dee and I are running away together."

"Huh?" Judy surfaced with a puzzled frown. "Oh. Well, you always did have the hots for her."

"Me and the entire lesbian nation. I don't know what she sees in you."

Judy slumped in the seat. "Ray, I have gained twenty-eight pounds. My breasts reach my knees and

I'm just about incontinent, not to mention the acne in surprising new places." Her voice quavered. "I do not need to feel insecure."

Oops. She'd broken one of the major rules of dealing with extremely pregnant women. Rayann quickly said, "I'm just teasing you, Jude, you know that."

"It's true. I don't know what she sees in me." Judy seemed desolate.

"Well, I never knew what Louisa saw in me..."

"Don't be silly." Judy looked at her as if the answer was obvious.

"I won't be if you won't be."

Judy half grinned. "Okay. You would have made a good therapist."

"Please. I'd be screaming *whiner* at my patients all the time."

"Not to mention you won't set foot inside a therapist's office."

Rayann tried to look as if she didn't understand Judy's meaningful stare. Judy still wanted Rayann to go to the grief counselor she'd recommended.

"I want you to make me a promise. Just one promise. I haven't asked anything of you and you have to humor a pregnant woman."

"That's emotional blackmail, Jude."

"Call a cop. Geez, Ray, one little promise."

"What?" Rayann sighed with all the weariness she could muster.

"I want you to do one of the steps in the book I gave you. Just one step. One little step. If it doesn't help, then I'll stop bugging you."

"Which one?"

"You pick."

"Oh, all right. Christ." Judy might be her oldest

and closest friend, but she was still a pain in the ass sometimes.

"By Sunday. When I see you at the grand opening I will want your assurance that you did it. You don't have to tell me about it, just that you did it."

"And you'll believe me?"

Judy gave her a long, level look. "I'm just trying to help Louisa rest in peace."

Rayann drew a ragged breath. "That's low."

"I'm desperate, Ray. You look like shit. I'll bet you aren't sleeping, and you're clearly not eating. I never asked exactly how you managed to hurt yourself with chisels you've been using for years, but I can guess. You have all the classic signs of depression and that's one of the stages."

"You don't understand." She stared out the window.

"Yeah, I have no experience with it at all. Forget about my degree and my umpteen years in practice. I'm going to break all the rules of therapy and be a friend. And as a friend I'm telling you that Louisa would be the first person to kick you in the hinder. She wouldn't like this, not at all."

That Louisa would deplore the state she was in was undeniable. She knew it as well as Judy did. But Louisa wasn't the one who had had to go on with living. A different kind of anger flickered and she clamped down on it. She would not be angry with Louisa. Louisa had not asked to get hit by a truck.

Dedric turned from the mailbox and looked quizzically in the passenger window. "You coming in?"

Judy opened the door and held out her hands. Dedric helped her up and kissed her the moment it was physically possible. Rayann kept the sigh to herself. Dedric was still head over heels for Judy.

She weathered the traffic from the Fillmore district toward the Bay Bridge. Two lanes of Gough were blocked, so it was slower than usual but she didn't mind. She was in no hurry to get home or anywhere else for that matter.

Traffic on the bridge picked up a little and she turned on the CD. The intricacies of Suzanne Ciani's *Velocity of Love* occupied her mind and she let the music and landscape flow past her in a blur of beauty that she hardly heard or saw. Louisa loved this song.

The pace picked up after Treasure Island and she gazed at the row of white container loaders at the Port of Oakland. One of them had recently been painted yellow and it really bothered her. At least the hills were unchanging. The Campanile still glistened in the setting sun. She liked this span of the bridge and didn't understand why some people called it ugly. They were going to replace the eastern span because the existing one wasn't earthquake-safe. Something else that wasn't staying the same.

She just needed everything to be the same for a while.

The sunset in the rearview mirror was incredible. She only noticed it because it was another beautiful sunset she wasn't watching with Louisa. Another day of emptiness. Another night of knowing the pain would never end. Rayann could almost feel the nuzzle of lips against her throat. She made herself a gin and tonic for dinner and cradled it on her chest as she lay in bed. She switched off the bedroom light and stared up at the moons and stars intertwined in the tapestry overhead. When she closed her eyes she could see the briar border of golden leaves and red roses against her eyelids. She inhaled, imagining firm lips grazing her ear. When would she stop longing? It didn't matter what the book Judy had given her about grief and grieving said. She was never going to stop feeling this way.

New Year's Eve morning, she wrapped herself in warm sweats, found her gloves and set out for a walk. She'd promised Judy she'd do just one thing from the book and this was it. The ice-edged wind blew her along the street and she welcomed the sunshine on her cheeks.

She checked her watch. She was right on time.

Her feet followed a path she had traced in her mind many times before. But until now, she had not actually walked it, not since then. At the corner of Lake Shore and Twentieth, she paused, let the light turn green, then stepped out into the six lanes of bustling boulevard. When she reached the fourth lane over, she stopped, checked her watch. On a brilliant, beautiful day, eight months and one week ago . . . at this very moment it had happened.

She shuddered all over, then broke out in a cold sweat, reliving not the moment of impact, but the shrill of the phone on her desk and the gravely phrased words of an Oakland police officer. Sweat poured down her back and she gasped for breath.

A honk forced her eyes open and she confronted the line of traffic that wanted to move forward. Her green light was long gone.

"What are you, crazy or something?"

"Wanna get yourself killed?" The cars burst forward as she made it to the opposite curb, accelerating hard as if to alleviate the annoyance of the drivers.

"One damn minute won't kill you," she muttered. What was one minute anyway? The difference between safety and death, she reminded herself.

She stumbled onto the walking path that circled the lake, a three-and-a-quarter-mile trek, and let herself get lost in memories again. Eight months since she had seen Louisa walk toward her and watched the line of her thighs brushing together. It just wasn't possible.

"Lady, out of the way."

She had come to a stop in the middle of the path, submerged in all the impressions of that horrible time. She was remembering things she hadn't noticed before — Teddy's grief, Danny's calm, her mother's steadfastness. And the source of her own guilt.

She sank down on the damp, grassy slope. *I didn't abandon you*. She closed her eyes and saw the flash of Louisa's warm smile.

She stretched out in the cold winter sun and let herself drown in the heat of the past. She curled up as the familiar longing seared through her. She pinned one of Louisa's arms and used her free hand to trail lazily the length of Louisa's torso. She kissed her fiercely and let her fingers tangle in the silky hair that greeted her. She could feel the prickle of the gray strands. She loved how they left her cheeks slightly raw, marked with proof that Louisa needed her, wanted her.

Even as she moved to take Louisa, Louisa's hand was there, hard between her legs, given more force by the knee behind it — and she melted. All over again, in a few fevered heartbeats. She gasped, let Louisa take her, held on, found herself enclosed by the curtain of Louisa's beautiful hair, gasping in their private world which held only the fierce strokes of Louisa's fingers and Rayann's aching body.

"More," she whimpered.

"Ma'am, are you okay?" A jogger was looking down at her.

She blushed and said, "I'm okay. Just a cramp."

"Oh, okay." He loped away and Rayann marveled at how people seemed so impersonal until she wanted only to be left alone. Then everyone was asking her if she was okay.

She finished her walk in the familiar daze, longing for Louisa with every step and unwilling to remember more. She took a deep breath before she opened the front door, just as she did every time she opened it. She still clung to the idea that she would get home and Louisa would be there.

I'll never let go of you.

The answering machine was flashing. Someone wanted something, wanted to make a date, wanted her to get out of the house.

"Hi, sweetie, it's Mom. Liman's does have an opening for art director. You should go for it with both hands. They could really use you, and you always said they were the type of firm you could really enjoy working in. It's a place where you could make partner while you were still young enough to enjoy it. Talk to you later."

Her mother was right. Liman's was a good firm for her. She liked their politics and their style. It was a small firm, nowhere as big as Tony's and nothing compared to the national firm her mother worked for, but that meant she could have an impact. She also had the resources to buy into a partnership if it was offered. It would be something to do with the money that was just sitting in the bank.

But it would mean getting up every day, finding the strength to leave the house when she kept thinking that if only she stayed home one more day Louisa would walk through the door. If she wasn't there when Louisa knocked then she really would be dead.

God, what an irrational thing to believe, she thought. She banged her head on the doorjamb. It hurt. "She's not coming back," she said fiercely to her reflection in the entryway mirror. "Get it through your head."

With shaking fingers she looked up the phone number for Liman's and placed her call. She remembered to turn on the fax machine, and a few minutes later it dropped the position details in her hand. The receptionist had recognized Rayann's name and had seemed a little flattered by her interest.

What did some receptionist know? She didn't know that the successful Rayann Germaine didn't go out of the house unless she had to. That Rayann Germaine made more dinners from gin than she would ever admit. She was flirting with alcoholism, and that was another thing Louisa would have hated.

I don't want to do this.

Louisa's voice was like a gong in her head. *You have to.*

It had been Louisa who had suggested that the bookstore wasn't enough use of Rayann's talents. It had been Louisa who had lovingly bullied and bolstered her ego until she put together a résumé and used her mother's contacts to get interviews in firms that never had to advertise openings.

Just like then, it was Louisa who made her turn on the computer and bang out a letter to Philip Liman. It was Louisa who reminded her where the stamps were. And it was Louisa who made her fumble in the freezer for a frozen dinner instead of in the cabinet for the Tanqueray.

I can't go on like this.

I wouldn't want you to.

She wrapped her arms around a pillow and fell asleep to Katharine Hepburn romping through *Bringing Up Baby*. She could hear Louisa's husky tones . . . "I can't give you anything but love, baby . . ."

8

Teresa checked her watch for the zillionth time. She had been standing in front of the party hall at the Hotel Regent for nearly forty minutes. The buffet dinner was well underway, the music had started, and there was no sign of Susan. She wondered if she should call or just accept the fact that Susan wasn't coming. She could not believe she was being stood up on New Year's Eve.

She showed her hand stamp to the woman who guarded the door and wandered back into the party. At the moment the music was swing and she wanted in the worst way to dance. But the place was full of couples. Couples to the left of her, couples to the right. Into the valley of singledom she rode.

She wasn't looking for a wedding. She just wanted a fun evening. Maybe a little passion of the unbridled variety. Was that too much to ask?

She caught a glimpse of herself in the mirrored wall. Was she a troll? She didn't think so. Her hair was newly done. The stylist had raved about how thick it was, and it did look good shorter in the back and stacked up a little on the back and side. It showed off the faint red tints amongst all the black. The new haircut combined with the tuxedo she'd rented even made her a little bit butch. So how come heads weren't turning? At least not the heads she wanted to turn. The hotel bellmen did not count.

She'd call. Maybe Susan was the type who ran late for everything.

She had nearly given up after six rings when she heard the receiver lifted. She didn't recognize the voice. "Is Susan there?"

"Nah, she took off for the weekend to ski. Who's this?"

"Um, well, I sort of had a date with her tonight."

The woman on the other end of the line hooted. "That'll be news to Susie's girlfriend. You must have made the date during their latest spat."

"I guess so. Thanks for the info."

She blinked back tears. Vivian at this very moment was probably boffing like a double-backed aardvark at Kim's place. What was she doing wrong? She'd been to the bar dressed to the nines, to the gay and lesbian center at the library sporting the latest lesbian romance under one arm. She ought to Day-Glo her forehead so that in lesbian light her forehead would announce, "Single! No U-Haul!"

Well, the ticket had been too expensive to waste. She drifted to the dinner buffet and helped herself to delicacies of the known and unknown variety. The salad looked like kale and arugala. She'd gotten used to the bitter flavor of arugala, but really — who had decided kale was food? She was frowning at it when the woman next to her said, "I hate it, too."

Teresa took in a pair of light-brown eyes surrounded by long black lashes. They were part of an olive-toned face that contained a very nice smile. Don't act desperate, she cautioned herself. "The first time I had kale in a salad I thought there was something wrong with it."

"Kale? I thought you were looking at the caviar."

"Caviar I can leave or take."

The woman peered at her salad. "What's kale?"

"I'm not sure. All I know is it makes my mouth go yuck." After a pause she added, "I'm Teresa Mandrell."

"Dawn Yahama. Are you here by yourself?"

"Unfortunately, yes. I got stood up."

"What an idiot. Her, not you. There's a table of singles over there." Dawn pointed. "Friendly group. There just happens to be an empty seat next to me." She raised her eyebrows with a suggestive wiggle.

The group at the single's table was indeed friendly, and after all the preliminaries of sharing where everyone worked and lived, Teresa found herself dancing with Dawn. The evening was not a total bust, she decided.

The music grew more frenetic toward midnight, reaching its crescendo during a twenty-second countdown to the new year. Mylar balloons cascaded from the ceiling until the floor was so thick with them that dancing became wading. The lights fell to a subdued sparkle. Dawn nuzzled her neck as they swayed to "Auld Lang Syne."

The nuzzling felt quite pleasant. Very pleasant. Teresa did some nuzzling of her own.

"I have a room," Dawn whispered.

Magic words, Teresa thought. "I think I'm just about done with dancing for the night."

"At least standing up."

Dawn was a good kisser. Just the right amount of pressure followed by a nip on Teresa's lower lip. Teresa responded with a hungry nibble. It felt wonderful when Dawn's arms slid around her waist.

They weren't alone in the elevator, but all the twosomes seemed to have the same agenda they did. The pheromone level was probably high enough to arouse a cadaver.

Dawn's palms were hard against her ribs as she stood behind Teresa. They exited by themselves on Dawn's floor and kissed their way to Dawn's room. Inside, it was a matter of moments before Teresa had Dawn's blouse unbuttoned.

A woman . . . Teresa felt like melting. The richness of skin, the texture of nipples — there was nothing that could compare to the feel of a woman's body against her own.

Dawn's hands were finished with Teresa's pants' button and zipper. They snaked their way under Teresa's pantyhose, and Teresa's entire body shivered deliciously. "Constant Craving" began to play in her head. Every nerve felt alive and aware that she was breast to breast with a soft and strong woman, k.d.

crooning in the background. It was so much better than in an alley with that woman —

Teresa froze. The crooning stopped. Where the hell had that thought come from?

"What's wrong?" Dawn's whisper brushed Teresa's ear in the darkness.

"Nothing," Teresa assured her. "Nothing at all."

"Let's get on the bed."

A new voice cut across the room. "That might be a little difficult since I'm in it." The bedside lamp came on. "Surprise, honey."

Teresa stared at the naked — and very angry-looking — woman in the bed, then at Dawn. Her libido had reached a nine on a scale of ten and it looked like it wasn't going to get to ten anytime soon.

Dawn looked like she was going to faint. "You weren't — you're supposed to be —"

Teresa addressed herself to a fickle God who had had just a little too much fun playing cosmic jokes on her lately. "I don't fucking believe this." She started buttoning.

The woman in the bed threw off the covers, revealing generously rounded hips and breasts. Teresa put her tongue back in her mouth. This was just not fair.

"I got back early, Dawn, *honey,* my faithful *love.* I told you I might. Who's this? Some hard-up bimbo looking for a quickie?"

"Excuse me?" Teresa's voice hit an octave she didn't know was in her range. "I didn't know she had a girlfriend."

The woman sneered. God, she had the kind of body Teresa loved — extremely squeezable. "I'll bet you didn't even ask."

"She was at the single's table!" Teresa gave Dawn a look that should have reduced her to cinders. "I am *not* a bimbo."

Dawn just stood there with her mouth open. She was such a good kisser, Teresa thought. *I'm screwed. I can't even remember the last time I had sex and I didn't even know it was for the last time ever in my entire life.*

She zipped up her fly with all the dignity she could muster and walked out the door. She took a cab home. She quickly realized that for whatever reason Vivian and Kim hadn't gone to Kim's place. Boffing like double-backed aardvarks was putting it mildly.

Maybe on her new salary she could afford a place of her own. Or better yet, she could rent a room in a nunnery. That way, there was a reasonable chance that "Oh, God" was actually addressed to a supreme being. The woman in the bed had pretty much been a supreme being. Dawn hadn't exactly been chopped liver either.

She had not thought the night could get worse, but a few minutes later she discovered that Vivian had taken the last of the batteries.

New Year's Day was a sale bonanza. Teresa drowned her frustrations in big discounts on shoes and jeans. She couldn't stay another minute in the apartment with Vivian and Kim making eyes at each other over their coffee. Loaded down with bags, she just made it to the IMAX theater in Yerba Buena in time to see the re-released *Chronos*. As she was leaving she bumped into one of the other museum assistants who had been let go and learned she was very fortunate to be working again so soon.

Comfortably clad in black leggings, scarlet cashmere sweater complete with a Peter Pan collar and Aldos, she reported to Diego Monday morning with two dozen muffins as requested. With an evil laugh, he gave her a huge stack of art boards covered in red corrections.

Settling in at her cubicle was easy. It wasn't that big. She clipped up her favorite picture of her dad and her framed Eugène Ionesco quote: *A work of art above all is an adventure of the mind.* Another minute or two to adjust the background colors on her computer display to her preferred settings and anyone observing her might think she'd been there for months instead of minutes.

The high ceiling and good lighting kept her from feeling boxed in and it didn't take long for her to catch on to the chat and mail functions of the computer. She was introduced at the staff meeting, greeted warmly, then everyone scurried to their own business. The atmosphere was a few notches below frenetic, but everyone seemed in a good humor.

When she got back to her desk she had an e-mail from Philip Liman titled, "Liman's Lands the Joe Camel Account." She read the message in horror, but then it dawned on her, given the peals of laughter emanating from all corners of the floor, that it was a joke.

She said over the cubicle wall to Diego, "I take it that we're not all going to be immediately receiving a hundred percent increase in salary and two free cartons of cigarettes every week?" In very small print, a footnote to a footnote announced, "Lung cancer is no longer covered by the company health plan."

Diego was still giggling. "I've been here six years and this is one of Philip's better holiday missives. Last year on April Fool's we had been bought by Microsoft."

She went to work with a smile on her face. As the first weeks of her new job went by the routine was punctuated by frequent fire drills — situations that needed immediate attention from a project team. She kept her head down and concentrated on learning the recently upgraded graphics program.

She was proofing a printout when her phone beeped that the intercom was open. "Hey, Teresa. We need you in conference room C — bring your sketch-pad."

Amy disconnected before Teresa could do more than stutter out, "Okay."

It was a most welcome interruption. Diego had not been kidding when he'd said he would dump all his shitwork on her. She was getting really fast at composing display art, adding text and zapping it to the printer. For several days she'd just done what was asked without really looking, but after a week and a half she felt as if she could evaluate what she was working on and give an opinion on it — a couple of times Amy had actually asked. She was really sorry that Amy's last day was tomorrow.

She settled into a conference room chair, glad that she knew everyone. Jena Davies was an account manager and Gene Huang was a copywriter. It looked like they were working on one of Jena's biggest clients, Ardley Foods. Display ads used in wholesaler's magazines were scattered around the table.

Amy picked up one, then let it slip through her fingers. "The cartoon image is just not working for them. I think we're relying too much on the idea that it conveys organic simplicity. It has no distinction. Teresa, what we want is something not cartoon but still not mechanically rendered."

"Like . . . children's drawings?"

"More sophisticated than that, but still looking illustrated by hand. Jena?"

"Let's see what it would look like." Jena had a dreamy British accent that was a sexy contrast to her dreadlocks.

Teresa pushed that thought back into the closet, where her libido was destined to stay forever. "Something easy — the sheaf of grain. You mean bold colors —" Her goldenrod pencil swept over the page. "— with soft lines." She used a light brown to differentiate the stalks, then charcoal to outline it. "Thicker lines is more childlike, but it's still sophisticated." It felt great to be using pencil and paper for a change.

"What do you think, Gene?"

"I'd do the same thing with the type. Use the same font we've always used but hand-lettered." Gene smiled at Teresa. "Could you do the Ardley name?"

Three shades of red and the same charcoal outline later, it was done.

Amy said, "We can go with this. Thanks, Teresa. Would you be up to doing all the boards? We'd need

them by . . ." She narrowed her eyes at Jena as if cal-
culating. "They'd have to be done by tomorrow morning, wouldn't they?"

Jena nodded reluctantly. "I'd say so. Otherwise we
can't run them by Philip before they go to the client.
I'm sorry, Teresa."

"I have no plans," Teresa said. "Let me run out
and get a big dinner and a really large supply of
chocolate. I could use the fresh air." It looked like
there were nine to ten display ads to do. Once she got
the color palette set up, they'd be straightforward
enough to sketch out on the computer's stylus pad.

"Thanks, Teresa." Amy checked her watch. "Lord,
I'm late for a meeting. Another ten bucks for Green-
peace."

Teresa skipped back to her cubicle. She didn't
mind the long night at all. It felt terrific to be a part
of the team.

The elevator had descended about two floors when
her mind registered the identity of the other occupant.
What on earth was that . . . that woman doing in the
building? As was typical, she was not taking any
notice of Teresa, as if Teresa wasn't even there.

She deliberately turned so that Rayann Germaine
could not ignore her. It was a breach of elevator eti-
quette, she knew. "Hi."

It was the eyes that shocked her most. As hateful
as her mocking gaze had been before, it had at least
been alive, filled with fire. The eyes that looked at
Teresa now were cold, extinguished. Then she took in
the pallor. The suit looked two sizes too large. Gone

were the full breasts she had been so close to taking into her mouth —

"Hi." The voice was the same. Slightly husky. Definitely off-putting.

She'd started a conversation, Teresa realized. And now there was nothing to do but blush and watch the floor indicators.

"Do you work for Liman's?"

Looking at Rayann was like looking into a black hole. Teresa could feel the pull of something dark and unhappy. The woman was miserable and yet she looked . . . composed. "In the art department."

The elevator ride ended, thank God. Several of the media buyers clumped on and Rayann was on the street before Teresa cleared the elevator. She looked after the rigid figure, walking upright as if in defiance of horrific weights. If Teresa wanted to illustrate *A Christmas Carol* she would use Rayann for a female Jacob Marley. But where had the chains come from?

Teresa dismissed the chance encounter as she savored a huge plate of pad thai liberally sprinkled with spiced peanuts. What did it matter to her if Rayann Germaine had business with someone at Liman's? It wasn't unheard of. Besides, she was so over that whole mess.

On the way back to the office she slipped into See's and bought three peanut crunches, two Victoria toffees and five Scotch kisses. The drugstore had peach Snapple in diet. It was so cold it had ice crystals in it. Perfect.

She set her goodies down next to her computer

and went in the direction of a general hubbub from the big conference room.

"What's up?" Mike Freeman occupied the third of three cubicles that made up the cluster she and Diego shared.

"They hired Amy's replacement. Philip was just giving us background, but I can't hear a word of it."

Teresa prickled all over. Oh no. No. It couldn't be.

"Did you get the name?" She was talking to Mike as if from the end of a tunnel.

"Ray something. But not a guy."

"Rayann Germaine." Christ on a cross.

"That's it. Rayann Germaine. I think Philip said she won a Clio. I would have thought we were low-rent for someone like that."

"So would I," Teresa murmured.

The thud from the other shoe dropping left Teresa feeling as if she'd just survived an earthquake.

After her final meeting at Philip Liman's, Rayann decided to stop in at her mother's. She called ahead to make sure her mother was home from work, but kept the reason for her visit a secret. She was going to be ecstatic, Rayann predicted.

She was. "Ray, I'm so happy for you!" The exuberant hug left Rayann gasping for breath. "I have a cheesecake — let's celebrate."

Jim was equally enthusiastic. "Should we open a bottle of wine?"

Rayann intercepted a look from her mother to Jim that said no. How worried they all must be, she thought. She hadn't been fooling anyone. "None for me," she said. "I've turned over a new leaf."

146

Her mother rushed away, but not before Rayann saw a shimmer of tears.

"I'm glad to hear that," Jim said quietly. "Your mother worries so."

Her mother wasn't the only one, obviously. She strove for a lighter tone. "You know what the worst part is? I have to confess to Judy that her silly grief therapy book worked." It hadn't been a panacea, but taking that one step of visiting the place where the accident happened had shattered her illusion of control. She had accepted that she was not, could not be in control all the time. The bouts of depression and anger were still frequent, but they were more manageable.

"Patrick's mother didn't die," Jim was saying. "But when she left me I went through some of the same stages. I remember that conventional wisdom was not to go through it alone, but I couldn't conceive how it was possible to do it any other way. Of course then I had to realize that I'd been a selfish bastard who didn't show wife or son anything but annoyed tolerance when they intruded on my work. Luckily, Pat forgave me. When he was older. And Ann doesn't put up with me at all when I'm in that mood."

"Mom can be an irresistible force sometimes."

Jim chuckled. "Sometimes?"

"Il Fornaio," her mother sang. "Chocolate New York style cheesecake. Raspberry coulis on the side."

"Take that away." Rayann pointed at the raspberry sauce. "Do not mess up my chocolate with fruit stuff."

"Oh pooh. You don't know what's good. When do you start?"

"Monday, bright and early. Amy Bledsoe is willing to stay on for a few extra days to clue me in. I think

147

I'll use these couple of days to find a new place to live."

"Maybe that's for the best," her mother said.

"We weren't there long enough for it to feel like home. And we chose it because it was close to the bookstore. It was ideal for us, but not right for just me." Her rationalizations sounded fine, but she felt a stab of guilt. She had been a long time dealing with the irrational feeling that if she moved, Louisa wouldn't know where to find her.

"Where are you thinking of moving to?"

Rayann took note of her mother's crossed fingers. She smiled reluctantly. "Back to the city."

"Yes!" Her mother did a double thumbs-up. "Jerry Ingram at work is selling his condo because he's moving to Marin. It's just south of Market with a view of the estuary. You can see Alcatraz from the balcony."

"I couldn't possibly afford something like that. Not if I want to hold on to what I have for a partnership buy-in at Liman's."

"Well, run the numbers. But mortgage rates have never been this low. You could walk to work from there. And to the new ballpark."

"Oh, now I see the interest."

Jim stifled a yawn. "I don't know where that came from."

Rayann immediately yawned. "Stop that. I have to get going, anyway. It's been a longer day than I'm used to. Thanks for the cheesecake, Mom."

"Anytime. Let's do lunch next week." Her mother beamed. "I've been waiting to say that to you again."

Let's do lunch, Rayann thought. She was back in the corporate world. And it felt okay.

*　*　*　*　*

Wallpapering is not particularly easy to do by your-self. Rayann knew the general steps, and they had chosen an easy-to-match pattern. It still took her most of a day to paper one wall. She was pleased when she was done. When she rehung the pictures the house would look more saleable.

It looks as nice as we thought it would.

A walk in the rain was a welcome break from some quick and dirty sponge painting to spruce up the kitchen. It wasn't far to Everett & Jones. She carried her barbecue home and once she was sated on ribs and potato salad, she called the broker who had helped them buy the house. It was still hard to accept condolences, and she preferred to avoid them as much as possible, but a good real estate broker is a good real estate broker, she told herself. The broker promised to drop by in the morning with the listing forms and agreements.

I've set it all in motion. I'm officially getting on with my life, she thought.

And I'm proud of you. Since taking the first step toward coping with her grief, Louisa had been speak-ing to her again. She knew that accepting her own wishful thinking as Louisa's presence was a step backward, according to the book. Well, the book was not perfect. She didn't believe that death was the end of life, not anymore. Louisa was with her and always would be. And that meant having spontaneous con-versations with her was perfectly sane.

The following morning she went to see the condo her mother had mentioned and made an offer. The location was great and always would be, from an investment perspective. It was a three-bedroom box in a building of boxes, but the light and view were definite pluses. At home again, she tackled the filthy condition of the bathroom with a great deal of bleach and energy. Louisa pointed out the corners she missed.

When she was too tired to clean she turned on her laptop instead of the television and wandered around the online message boards, then dipped into a couple of the Web sites that did advertising reviews. She'd missed some major campaigns, and it looked like the trend of paying megabucks to superstars to sell products was waning. Only sports figures with sporting goods were a sure match. The trend seemed to be turning toward spokespeople the buyer identified with rather than looked up to.

Her browser locked up three times trying to load the site of one of Liman's biggest clients, so she gave up for the night.

She changed the sheets, scrubbed herself pink in a hot shower, then curled up with the electric blanket on. She would keep the bed and the tapestry, she thought. The memory of waking up for the first time under it was a sweet one. She had added her own carvings in the fired olive wood of the posts, echoes of the emerald runes working in the tapestry's zodiac circle. She would keep the bed. But she could not think that in some very distant future she might share this view with someone. That she would even want to was inconceivable. Her body still belonged to Louisa as surely as if Louisa had marked every cell with an *L*.

L could stand for lesbian, Louisa whispered.

Oh hush, Rayann thought. That wasn't Louisa, that was just her pesky sex drive in the "on" position as always. Rayann's chief problem, Judy had informed her after two years of psych classes, was her body's willingness to engage in meaningless sex when her mind was stuck in the Victorian era. Therefore she fell in love with every woman she had sex with.

Which was not true, Rayann thought. When she'd been resisting her unrelenting lust for Louisa she'd had a very pleasing dalliance with a woman, no strings. And she'd been well in love with Louisa even when she thought there was no way Louisa would ever touch her.

That first time — the memory of it washed over her. Christmas Eve, ten years ago. Kisses that came out of nowhere, the savage ache of her body, the burn of Louisa's jeans against her bare thighs. She had felt naked, open, raw with need. Louisa had quenched it all, understanding what Rayann wanted more than Rayann did.

She would not find that again.

She abruptly remembered the woman in the alley behind that bar she'd wandered into. God, she'd been so drunk. She had enough distance now to understand why she'd let it happen . . . why she had wanted it to happen. What she remembered of it sent her pulse racing.

She turned her face into the pillow and opened the memory of fingertips tracing her spine, parting her thighs, teasing her breasts. The memory was a sweet solace now and she drifted into a more restful sleep than she had had in months.

9

The inevitable summons came. Teresa had been dreading it all week.

She hadn't been at work the first day that Rayann took over for Amy — a day off in return for the all-nighter she'd done on the Ardley display ads and for two other really late nights. Then Rayann and Amy had spent one day in seclusion. Going over client backgrounds, probably.

Pressing business had kept Rayann in her office

most of yesterday, but apparently she was wanting to meet with all of her staff, one by one.

You're not the same person, Teresa reminded herself. Just don't fly off the handle. You really like this job. Diego said she was really nice. Give her a second chance. Third chance.

She continued the pep talk all the way to the office door. Then she rapped on the doorjamb and went in.

"You must be Teresa," Rayann said. She rose to shake Teresa's hand, then settled into her chair again.

She really does not remember me. Not from the old job, not from the alley, probably not even from the elevator.

Rayann went on, "We met in the elevator, didn't we?"

"That's right. I didn't know you worked here — that you were going to be working here." Okay, so she had registered, at least on some level, in the elevator.

"A surprise to me, as well. I understand you've only been here a short while, too."

"Since New Year's."

"And yet, look at this mountain of work." Rayann gestured at the Ardley Foods display ads. "I don't know if anyone has told you this lately, but true artists in commercial art are getting rare. People with talent are going directly to commercial art trade school without stopping to develop their own art-for-arts-sake talent first. One can hardly blame them — a paycheck is a paycheck."

"I did a year at the Sorbonne." Maybe that would spark a memory of their earlier clash. "My grand-

153

mother lives in France, which helped a lot." Of course remembering the first time they'd met might make Rayann remember the second, and Teresa did not think their working relationship would be helped by memories of that alley.

Rayann's reaction was completely different this time. "I saw that on your résumé. I'd have given my eyeteeth to do that. But wood scuplting is not exactly haute art, if you know what I mean."

Where on earth had this woman come from? Who had stolen the Queen of Mean Rayann Germaine and left this . . . *nice* person in her place? "It's good to feel as if I have something unique to contribute."

"I understand that feeling all too well. Well, I didn't have a specific agenda. I just wanted to get a chance for a normal conversation with everyone before it gets insane. More insane, rather."

The meeting was over, which was no problem. She'd expected the worst, but she was just really confused. Maybe Rayann was manic depressive. Maybe she was a manic depressive alcoholic. A manic depressive alcoholic lesbian who had stopped taking her steroids.

"What did you think of her?" Diego's network message popped up on her screen. Everyone preferred them when you wanted to have a private conversation, something not possible in the all-cubicle setup.

"I thought she was nice, like you said," Teresa typed back. No need to tell Diego that they'd met before. That she had in fact thrown her job in Rayann's face, then attempted to seduce her. Put that way it didn't exactly do Teresa credit. But it hadn't been all her fault. Rayann *had* been a bitch to her.

She went back to work on her latest stack of

display ad edits. They were tiresome, but she could do them in her sleep now. Clip, adjust, size, type, print. Next.

She heard the thump of running footsteps and popped up to see who was going where. Jena Davies and Tori Raguza were hustling across the floor from the elevators to Rayann's office.

Other people were prairie-dogging, and Diego said irritably, "What's going on?"

"Looks like a fire drill," Mike said. "Not me this time. No way. I got tickets to the opera."

Rayann came out of her office and smiled when she saw all the heads looking expectantly in her direction. "It's a fire drill," she announced, raising her voice. "Anyone who has no private life planned for the next forty-eight hours raise your hand. I need video, sound and art."

Video? Teresa's hand shot in the air. She was dying to work on a video project. Across the cubicles, Teresa saw Jim Dettman's hand go up. Good — Jim was reputed to be a video god. Tony Green came out of the break room saying, "Tony is your man for sound."

Henry was behind Tony. "Conference C is all cleaned up. I'll bring coffee." He pulled a fireman's hat into view and put it on, smiling broadly when everyone laughed.

I like this place, Teresa thought. *Let's see if I can survive working with her.*

Rayann had shed her jacket. The extent of her weight loss was more obvious — Teresa could hardly believe it. Maybe she had been ill. There seemed to be plenty of charm on the surface, but what had happened to make the interior so cold?

155

None of your business, she thought. She put her sketchpad and pencils on the table and noticed that Jim had brought one as well.

"I suppose I didn't need this," Jim said, indicating his pad. "I don't do it near as good as you."

Tori automatically said, "Nearly. Nearly as good."

Jena was saying to Rayann, "I've already sent an alert over to media to pick up the spots." She turned to the rest of them. "This is really very exciting. Halon Technologies is a small client that we've been working with for a couple of years. Mostly little mailers and shareholder brochures because they haven't had a product to push. For the last two months we've been hammering out the media campaign for when their first product gets FDA approval and rolls out. That was supposed to happen this fall. They got FDA approval *today*."

Tori, whose primary work was copywriting, said, "Fortunately all of the legal disclaimer work is done. We also have the video spots planned, but they're live-action. Halon still wants to go with that plan in its entirety, but we can't bring it to market in less than two weeks without its looking like a rush job. So the client agrees we should complete the original plan properly, another two months, because when you're selling medicine you have to look competent."

Rayann chimed in. "So Halon wants to do a series of information spots on the news networks to fill the gap. The spots are aimed at potential users and their doctors. Because they're going to market early, they're willing to spend some major dollars on prime-time spots. CNN, HNN, MSNBC, Fox and major-market number-one news shows. That's a lot of exposure, and what we put out there must look competent and poised."

Jim steepled his fingers. "So no live action? Text on a background?" He glanced at Tony. "Voiceover?"

"Tony approves of voiceover."

Tori pursed her lips. "Tony, buy a pronoun."

"No bickering," Rayann said. She glanced at Teresa. "Any thoughts?"

"I have thoughts," Teresa said slowly. "I believe I'm probably thinking what all the people who will be watching this commercial will be thinking."

There was a silence, then Rayann said, "And that is?"

"What the hell is the product?"

Rayann blinked, then burst into laughter. "I have no the hell idea! Oh my God!" She laughed as if she hadn't done so in a long time. Teresa had to consciously shake the happy sound of it from her ears.

Through her chuckles, Jena said, "I rather left that out, didn't I? Well, if you know the Halon account, you know what they've been working on — inhalable insulin, just like asthma medicine. For approximately sixty percent of insulin-dependent diabetics, it means an end to needles."

"Wow," Teresa said. "That's really big."

Rayann wiped away a tear. "So what are your thoughts now?"

"Obviously it'll need to be serious, but that doesn't mean boring," Teresa said. "I think that coloration can change the whole mood. This is something to celebrate, after all."

Jim leaned forward. "How about going from black and white to color in the background. And have the voiceover go from pedantic to excited?"

"That sounds good," Rayann said. "Maybe not that dramatic with the voiceover — remember, there's all the medical disclosures to be read — but I like where we're going. It'll produce fast and we can surprise the client with something for over the weekend."

Jena emptied the file on the media campaign onto the table. "This is what we have to work with. The client promises they won't do fifteen levels of review so we can get this on as soon as possible. We just have to stick within the groundwork we've already done. Here are the legal disclaimers." She pushed a sheet at Tony. "And here are the keywords, the color swatches. These are the performers lined up for the live action commercial." She tapped one of the head shots. "He has an interesting voice. A little gravelly, just a little. And he's local. With any luck at all we could have him in for recording tomorrow."

In the end, Teresa didn't have a lot to do except watch and learn. Jim appreciated her perspective on the color shading and the placement of the product against text. By midnight he had the product video on bluescreen done. Being the least engaged, Teresa was the one who took a cab to an all-night deli for provisions. Even with curb-to-curb service from the cab driver, she got rained on. She kept leaving her umbrella at home because sometimes it was hard to tell fog from rain clouds.

She carried Rayann's sandwich into her office, only to stop short when she realized the other woman had fallen asleep on the little couch in the corner. Even in sleep the tense expression and cool withdrawal hadn't changed.

Teresa took a moment to study the photographs that had been set out on the credenza. She recognized the man in one of them — he'd been sitting next to Rayann when Teresa and Vivian had seen them at the Lace Place. There was a group shot which included that gorgeous redhead and her girlfriend, obviously taken pre-pregnancy. Another picture had to be of her mother, though there was little resemblance. She was very striking to look at. Thick, black and silver hair was blowing in the wind over a green hillside.

Something about the woman's steady gaze reminded Teresa of her grandmother. Lord, that woman was irascible. She'd agreed to let Teresa stay with her while she went to school in Paris. Teresa had been grateful until she had realized her father's assessment of her grandmother's temper was not just a mother-in-law thing. She really was that bad. She was at war with the world over everything. The bread was not fresh enough, the prices too high and worst of all, she had only one grandchild because Teresa's mother had had the bad manners to contract a fatal case of food poisoning when Teresa was two. Teresa was blameless in that, her grandmother allowed, but Teresa's father was a *trou du cul*. Teresa had asked another student to translate. *Trou* meant hole. *Cul* at its most polite meant buttocks. A day hadn't passed that her grandmother didn't call someone a *trou du cul*.

The woman pictured on Rayann's credenza did not have her grandmother's unhappy network of frowning wrinkles, however, nor her thin lips. She didn't look quite old enough to be Teresa's grandmother's age, either. She looked as if her life was as complete and full as she could make it. It was in the angle of her neck, the way she lifted her face to the wind. She had probably been a great mother. Of course never having had one, Teresa wasn't sure what exactly a great mother was. Sometimes she wondered what it would have been like. But the fact was that her father had been good enough for two parents.

He hadn't known anything about tampons but he had read the boxes with her. When he'd given her the last in a series of talks about sex, and how not having it was the classy choice for a girl her age, he'd given her condoms and said he trusted her to be an adult but he didn't trust teenage boys; after all, he'd been one once upon a time. He'd actually seemed relieved a year later when she'd told him that she felt "that way" about other girls. When her very first girlfriend had dumped her during her freshman year in college, he had been there offering hot fudge sundaes and sage advice about fish and seas. He was a great dad. She hadn't told him so recently. She'd have to rectify that as soon as possible.

Teresa shook herself out of her pensive mood and left the sandwich and cup of soup on the desk. She took Jim his food in the small video room and while they both ate, she showed him the color shift she could produce via computer. It was nothing fancy.

Tony wandered in, pastrami sandwich in one hand, printouts in the other. "Did you know that one of the side effects of this stuff is death?"

Jim scoffed. "We have to say 'death'? In a commercial?"

"Apparently so. The message of the legal disclaimers is that this stuff should be strictly supervised by a physician."

"Well, that makes sense," Teresa said. "Insulin can kill you."

"Tony thinks that when a commercial says our product can kill you the product is what dies."

Rayann had slipped in. "I'll talk to legal about it tomorrow. I don't see why we can't substitute 'life-threatening' for 'death.' " She rubbed her eyes. "The couch in my office is fair game for anyone who wants to catnap."

"Jena's crashed on the one in the break room," Tony said. "Tony will take dibs on Rayann's."

"I woke up because Tori buzzed me. She's got the copy ready. Thanks for the chow, by the way. The soup was exactly what I needed."

Rayann and Tony headed for the conference room while Jim overlaid the product shot from the blue-screen onto the deep gray that opened the spot. Teresa set the computer to transition from gray to a vivid blue several tints lighter than the Halon logo. "Thirty seconds starts now."

They watched the colors mutate. Halfway through, Teresa stopped it. "It's getting to blue by removing black. I want it to actually get there by going to deep purple, then remove the red. Just a sec."

"That makes a difference," Jim said, when the colors started to shift. "Before, it seemed to take forever to change."

"And right about here — in logo blue outlined in white — we'd see the phrase 'As easy as breathing,' then 'Halon Technologies.' "

"Let's run it one more time and I'll record. We could be done in an hour."

"Cool." She quickly typed the text in Halon's preferred font, and loaded up the TIFF of their corporate name spelled out. She added them to the computer display starting at second twenty-six, just before the final fade to white.

Jim took the cassette to the conference room and Teresa's eyes drooped. A catnap would be a big help. Jena was nowhere in sight and Tony had opted for the larger sofa in the break room. Tony should tell Tony that Tony snored.

She settled onto the little sofa in Rayann's office. As she closed her eyes she thought that never in a million years would she have predicted this end to the day. The faint hint of some scent prickled her nose and when she recognized it she turned into a great big goosepimple. She had smelled it before, on Rayann's skin.

Now, cut that out, she told her nose. There was absolutely nothing productive to be gained from it.

Whispered fumbling. Oh . . . soft. Not soft. Hard. Shit, she was waking up . . . oh, that was not fair. Teresa rubbed her eyes. Even her dreams were coitus out-of-luckus.

It was the phone buzzer that had disturbed a really great dream. To her chagrin, Rayann was at her desk, looking as if she'd been there for some time. She was talking quietly, and mouthed "Sorry" at Teresa.

Teresa swabbed her cheek. She'd even been drooling. How embarrassing.

The clock said it was almost five. She'd had more

sleep than everyone else, she realized. She got up as if she woke up in other people's office every day.

"We're getting together again in the conference room," Rayann said, as Teresa was heading for the door. She had finished her call. "That was Henry. He said his mother will make us a coffee cake for breakfast if we want it."

"Henry's mother is an amazing cook. I hope you said yes." Teresa ran her tongue over her teeth. Yuck.

"I said yes. And I asked him to pick up some Egg McMuffins for protein. You want some gum?"

Teresa smiled without showing her teeth. "Yeah. For everyone else's sake. I keep forgetting to bring a toothbrush for these wonderful all-nighters."

They walked together toward the conference room. Everyone was delighted to hear of Henry's mother's coffee cake in their future except Tori, who looked as if she'd just been poisoned. "Who made this coffee?"

"Tony made the coffee," Tony said irritably.

Tori snapped back, "When you see Tony tell him he makes shitty coffee."

"No bickering," Rayann said. "Let's see what we have."

Tori passed out the copy. "Tony has rehearsed it a couple of times to get it in the time frame. Since we're going with a male voice it'll be better to hear it done by a man now."

They were still adjusting the timing of the copy-reading when Henry arrived with the promised coffee cake and a sack of breakfast sandwiches. He quickly departed to make a fresh pot of coffee.

With food in their stomachs, everything seemed to click. Tori rearranged a sentence and they found two more seconds they badly needed. By the time the rest of the office arrived they were all hopeful that Philip would approve right away.

People began clamoring for Rayann's attention on other matters, but she rejoined them when Philip popped down to see the final result, which Jim had just remastered onto production-quality videotape.

Philip was pleased and a little sigh of happiness ran through everybody. "This is great teamwork, and they're not expecting this until tomorrow. Let's surprise them by making the evening news tonight. My sister is diabetic — she's going to be thrilled beyond belief."

Jena, looking as weary as Teresa felt, took the final tape to the client and Rayann gave the rest of them the choice of going home then or taking Friday off. Teresa opted for the Friday. Maybe she could find a cheap fare down to L.A. to see her dad for a three-day weekend. Of course he and Melanie could have plans. If she stayed home she could get out, try to have something like a life. Meet somebody. Have some fun. Sure, she thought. *Women just fall into your lap, uh-huh.*

Later in the day, her nose was just inches off her keyboard as she pecked out a text change on a display ad. She straightened up when Rayann leaned into her cube.

"I just wanted to say good work last night. The client loved it. It starts airing this evening during the eight o'clock hour on CNN."

"That's terrific. Sleep is where I'm headed tonight, so I'll probably miss the debut."

"You and me both —" Rayann broke off, looking

puzzled. She put her hand in the pocket of her skirt. "Oh my. I forgot that was in there." She pulled out a small object with a guilty smile, as if the vibration had felt a little too good. "One of those vibrating pagers. I'm carrying it around because a friend of mine is pregnant and I'm the backup." She glanced nonchalantly at the display. "Hospital." Her smile froze. "Oh my God. Oh my God. I have to go. Um. I have to go. See ya!" She fled toward her office and a few minutes later toward the elevator.

Teresa sat there with the funniest sensation in the pit of her stomach. For just a moment Rayann's entire being had changed. The coiled purpose that she had exuded the first time Teresa had met her suddenly glowed in full force.

She exhaled noisily. She'd never felt this mixture of butterflies and creepy tickles before. She shook her hands as if that would make it stop.

She did *not* want to know what had caused it. She did not want to go on experiencing it. She wanted it to go away. Rayann Germaine was not in the least bit attractive and whatever this feeling was had nothing to do with her.

Period.

End of story.

Finito.

Crap.

"Just give me the goddamned drugs!" Judy had Rayann's shirt sleeve clutched in one hand and the hospital bed rail in the other.

"The anesthesiologist is on the way," Rayann soothed. "Dee will be here in a little bit. Why don't you try the nitrous again?"

"It makes me dizzy." Judy gasped as she sank back on the bed with a moan.

The midwife looked up from her conversation with the delivery nurse. "Things are really progressing quickly, Judy. That's why it hurts. Fast hurts more, but it doesn't last as long. This baby wants into the world."

Judy gave a weak smile. "I'm sorry I yelled. I didn't know what to expect, and if we're just getting started and it hurts that much, I want drugs."

"Your contractions are very strong," the midwife said. "You didn't get any warmups to give you a sense of perspective. I want to check your cervix again because I suspect the contractions are very productive, given the pain you're in."

Judy closed your eyes. "Thank you for not calling it discomfort."

The delivery nurse laughed. "Childbirth is not uncomfortable. It hurts. But it's the best kind of hurt you'll ever experience. Lie back, please."

The midwife was quick. She was grinning widely when she removed her fingers. "My dear, you are six centimeters and climbing. We're having a baby. How long until Dee gets here?"

Rayann welcomed the surge of adrenaline those words gave her. Lack of sleep was making her punchy. "Soon, I hope. She'll kick herself if she misses it."

"I'll kick her butt all the way to Canada if she misses it," Judy snapped.

The midwife told the delivery nurse to bring the

delivery cart. She turned back to Judy. "This is going to be uncomfortable — really, just uncomfortable. I'm going to see if I can feel the baby's position. If it's head-down I'll attach a fetal monitor. The last ultrasound had it head-down and we'll hope that all this activity hasn't change that."

"Wait," Judy said. "Here comes another one."

Something was different about this contraction. Judy's entire body tensed and Rayann grabbed one flailing hand and put her arm around Judy's shaking leg. "I want to push." There was a desperate edge to her voice.

"I'm not surprised," the midwife said. "Don't push. Judy!" She shook Judy's other leg. "Don't push now."

"Candle-blows." Rayann thought she was going to hyperventilate as she demonstrated. "Please, Judy. Don't push. You're not dilated enough. Remember the class? If you push now it's going to hurt like hell and you don't have any drugs yet. The baby needs more room. Candle-blows. Come on. Do it with me."

She had Judy's attention. Judy began to puff as if she was blowing out a candle and the midwife said, "That's so much better. That's excellent, Judy. There, it's easing up now. The baby is head-down and face-down — the best of all possible positions. The monitor is on now."

The delivery nurse switched on a machine and turned it so Judy could see the digital display. "There's the heartbeat. Fast and steady, just the way we like it."

Judy was drenched. Rayann offered her apple juice and ice. They'd been joking earlier about how women had had babies in the fields and survived, but Rayann didn't feel like laughing now. She had had no idea. She knew Judy as well as she would know a sister. And she'd had no idea that Judy could be so strong.

The door opened and Dee rushed in. She was still in uniform, but a change of clothes was in the hospital bag Judy had brought with her. She bent over Judy's head, pressing her cheek to Judy's. "I got here as soon as I could. I was in court. Can you believe this baby's timing?"

"Just preparing us for the future," Judy said. Color was back in her face and half the tension went out of her body.

"Ain't that the truth? I gotta change, honey. And I have to find a place to lock up my gun. I don't want to have to worry about it."

"I'm fine," Judy said. "Drugs are on the way, I'm told."

Rayann started to assure Dedric that she would stay as long as she was needed when Judy gasped that another contraction was starting.

Dedric joined the chorus of voices reminding her not to push. Everyone except the delivery nurse was doing candle-blows to set the example.

When the contraction eased Dedric's pallor surpassed Judy's. "Is that normal?" She turned her panicky gaze on the midwife.

"Perfectly normal," the midwife assured her. The on-duty resident also nodded. He'd slipped in a few minutes earlier and stayed out of the way. Rayann knew he was required to be there by hospital rules, but it was obvious he knew that the midwife was in complete control of the situation.

"Christ, honey." Dedric smoothed Judy's brow. "I had no idea you were so butch."

Judy laughed weakly, then sniffed back tears. "Go get out of that damned uniform."

"Yes, ma'am. Don't have a baby while I'm gone, please."

The delivery nurse suggested the locked medicine closet for Dedric's gun. When Dedric came back she was in sweats, and her red hair was down from the efficient ponytail she favored for work. For once she looked human, Rayann thought.

Even though she had missed more than half the childbirth classes, Rayann knew Dedric had made sure that she and Judy practiced and trained on their own. Rayann didn't interfere with the synergy they had going. It reminded her of the way she and Louisa had worked together — almost wordless. A gesture could be an entire conversation.

The anesthesiologist arrived with two medical students in tow. Rayann watched with queasy fascination as a catheter was inserted into Judy's spine. Within moments, Judy said she felt a flush of numbness.

"Try moving your legs," the midwife suggested.

Judy raised them slowly. "It's difficult, but I can still feel them."

"That's perfect. You're going to be able to push and most of the contraction pain will be blocked. Rest in between as much as you can. Drink some more juice and then I'll check your cervix again."

No one said anything about her having to leave now that Dedric was there, so Rayann went around to the other side of the bed and tried not to get in the way.

The midwife pronounced it time to push. "I want two pushes per contraction, that's a quick count of ten each."

Already Judy was listening better. Clearly, her world had been reduced to what was happening in her pelvis and to the sound of Dedric's voice.

Rayann counted along with Dedric. "Breathe in, out, in, now push. One, two, three, four, five, six, seven, eight, nine, ten, breathe out. In, out, in, now push." She counted ten, quickening her pace with Dedric. Judy's exhale was raspy and Rayann quickly arranged the juice so Judy could sip.

"That was excellent," the midwife announced.

"I can't imagine doing that without the epidural," Judy said weakly. "I wanted to do it naturally."

Dedric smoothed her forehead. "I know you did, but it doesn't matter how the baby gets here."

"Another one's coming," Judy said. She pushed the juice away. She clutched Dedric's hand and gave Rayann a ragged smile. "No rest for the weary."

Rayann was swaying on her feet before she realized that Judy had been pushing for nearly an hour. She felt as if she was coming up for air. She had been focused on the baby's monitored heartbeat. It was so much faster than Louisa's had been. For a moment she was back in Louisa's hospital room, then the sound of Dedric's voice roused her from the empty pain.

"I know you're tired, baby, I know you are. But you can do it. One more push. Let's take it one at a time."

Judy pushed away Dedric's hand, then grabbed for

it the next instant. "I can't do it without you. Oh God, another one."

Like a thunderclap, Rayann had the first creative urge she'd felt in a long, long time. Her neck prickled with cold sweat as her heart raced. She was exhausted and exhilirated at the same time. She wanted to sketch them, but had no paper. If Judy hadn't forbidden it, she would have taken a picture for the memory. It was the way Dedric's neck was arched as she bent over Judy, the coil of their hands just below where Dedric's lips brushed Judy's ear as she counted. Judy's face was grooved with strain and determination . . .

Rayann was so caught in the tableau that she didn't at first register the midwife's excited cry. "You're crowning. That's it, I have a shoulder. Both shoulders! What a beautiful baby!"

Dedric burst into tears while Judy sobbed for breath. The midwife quickly placed the baby on Judy's chest.

It was a girl. Judy had told her that artificial insemination resulted in ninety percent boys.

"She's twice a miracle, now," Dedric said. She was still crying.

"Three times," Judy said. "She made you cry. I've never seen you cry before."

The tiny life gave a throaty yell. Right before Rayann's eyes she changed from a purple-skinned, Crisco-coated, *X Files*-looking alien to a bundle of infant girl. The skin tone was already flushing from purple to pink. The silvery blue eyes opened as her mother's chest provided both warmth and the familiar *lub-dub* she'd been hearing for the last nine months. She quieted with a little sigh.

The midwife offered Dedric the scissors to cut the cord. "It doesn't hurt, really. Between the two clamps."

"Welcome to the world, little one," Judy said, then she put a hand on her abdomen. "Oh, what's happening?"

"The afterbirth," the midwife reminded her. "The nurse is going to take the baby to the warmer and do her vitals while you push this out."

"More pushing? I can't." Judy's head fell back with a whimper.

"This is easy. Then I'll do just a little stitching. You'll be glad you had the epidural because by the time it wears off I'll be all done. You might want to have some more juice now."

"What's her name?" Rayann demanded. Why was no one sharing this very important piece of information? "I want to know my goddaughter's name."

Dedric ruffled the mass of black hair. "Joyner for Jackie Joyner-Kersee and Melissa for Judy's mother and Melissa Etheridge. And we're going to combine our last names from Kendall and Denton to Kent. So she will be Joyner Melissa Kent."

"What a regal name," Rayann said. "It carries the tradition of women athletes in your name."

"Joyner is a little prettier than Dedrickson."

Judy sniffed. "Dedrickson is a lovely name. A bit of a mouthful for a first name, but still lovely."

Dedric was smoothing Judy's forehead. It took only a little pushing until the afterbirth appeared and Judy closed her eyes. "I want to sleep for a week."

The midwife chuckled. "Sleep's over, Judy."

As if to confirm that, Joyner Melissa Kent wailed from the warming table.

"You can get out the camera now, Ray." Judy was watching Dedric hurry to the warming table.

Her photography was not anything special, but Rayann knew that the snap she got of Dedric offering her little finger to Joyner to clasp would be one they would cherish forever. It was an astonishing thing — before her eyes a baby had come alive and two of her closest friends had transformed.

As tired as she was she spent forty minutes with a sketchpad at home, trying to catch the essence of what she had witnessed before it was lost to sleep. She was out of practice — nothing looked quite right.

Unable to hold her head up any longer, she oozed into bed. Teresa from work would be able to draw it right, she thought. She had gifts Rayann could envy.

10

"I guess I would say that no two days are the
same." Teresa let the high-school student scribble
more on his notepad. "The pace can be frenetic but
the atmosphere is creative. And nothing stays the
same. I don't know, maybe that's just my effect on
places. Liman's hasn't reorganized the management
structure in years, but they just did it yesterday. I
have a new boss and my old boss was promoted. And
she just got here like, eight weeks ago."

"Do you make a lot of money?"

"Enough," Teresa said. "Not as much as at other

agencies. I mean, a commercial artist can go right to work for lots of agencies and probably make more. But as someone else who works here said, I don't have to use my best creative ideas to sell cigarettes to kids."

She answered a few more questions and then saw the kid to his next interview. She liked talking to a young person about what she did. Rayann had set everything up through the closest public high school.

She resisted the impulse to pop her head into Rayann's office and tell her that she thought the interviews were a great idea. Rayann was no longer her direct boss. The art department had been broken into three areas — art, video and sound. Those departments now all had new heads, promoted from within. Combined with copywriting, they were all managed by Rayann as the company's first creative director. It was how most ad agencies were organized on the creative side. Liman's had been an anomaly, maybe because Amy and Philip had liked it that way.

Rayann had also brought in a major new client, a regional chain of hardware stores. Their work was already spread throughout the department. The local business trade paper had covered "Liman's New Face" in the most recent issue. Teresa had snagged the front page for herself, thinking she might send it to her father. She smoothed Rayann's picture, then folded the page into her backpack.

There was no coffee, and Henry was gone for lunch. She had once made more while he was gone, but the invectives against whoever the idiot was that had messed with the coffee kept her from ever doing that again.

She decided to go out for a Snapple. She'd brought

her lunch because she wanted to save up for her own place, but one Snapple wouldn't make or break a security deposit plus first and last months' rent.

"Teresa, hang on."

She turned toward the sound of Jim's voice — he was just leaving Rayann's office.

"What's up?" Jim was just as easy to work with as a boss as he had been as a coworker.

"The video shoot for the hardware ad — they're redoing the entire storyboard. And it needs to be done fast because the technicians and talents are just standing around getting paid for nothing."

"Do we need to work tonight?"

"No. You, Tori and Rayann need to get on a plane to Phoenix. That's where they're shooting — and losing money. You're on a flight in about ninety minutes. No time to go home first."

"Crap." Her jeans hadn't been precisely clean when she'd grabbed them that morning.

"You do have about thirty minutes before the cab comes to take you all to the airport. Ray said to get yourself a change of clothes from whatever source and she'll reimburse you. Within reason, of course. Tori has probably already hit the shops."

"Casual Corner on Kearny. I'm there." She scooped her paperback, keys and wallet into her backpack, then pulled her laptop out of its docking station. She zipped it into its case and scooted down to the street. A sudden business trip was a nuisance — and an exciting opportunity.

It was probably a heck of a lot warmer and dryer in Phoenix. She bought a pair of chinos, a layered Henley top, undies and socks. She spied Tori waiting at the curb when she turned the corner. Tori was laden with a Macy's bag, her commuting satchel and laptop case. She was breathing hard.

"I ran all the way back because the charge card authorization was down. It took forever. Henry was just here. He said Ray is on her way down."

"Does this happen a lot?"

"Well, I've been in this business a little over eighteen years and no, it doesn't happen a lot. But with big, new clients anything is possible."

"What did you do before advertising?" Tori looked well into her fifties.

"I was a housewife. I have three beautiful children — the youngest is about your age, I'd guess. When their father paid off the last of his law school loans he decided someone younger was better suited to host his clients."

"That sucks." Thank you, God, she thought, for making me a lesbian.

"It wasn't fun. He could afford to buy the kids' affection every other weekend and I got to be the one they hated for enforcing rules like curfews. Now that the kids are older they like their father a great deal less, so I guess I won in the end." She sighed.

"But it wasn't a war you wanted to wage."

"No, not at all. It was years before I stopped hoping we would reconcile. I loved the jerk." She shrugged. "I have no idea why I'm telling you all of this."

"I asked. I'm nosy."

"You're a good listener."

"I don't know about that. I have two ears like everybody else." Teresa laughed awkwardly.

Tori was serious. "No, I noticed it in meetings. Believe me, I've been in brainstorming meetings where everyone wants red and the artist is an artist and keeps picking up a green pencil. You don't do that. You listen. You synthesize. You are very good at it."

Teresa ducked her head. She was not used to such lavish praise. "Thanks. I'm not sure it's all that special —"

"You're just like my daughter. I know she learned her self-esteem problems from me, because for a long time I thought I deserved to be cast off like a used coffee filter. She never believes praise."

"Okay, I'll try hard to believe it."

Tori was warming up to her theme. Teresa had to admit she liked it. "Remember the RTR session? Their first display ad. We were done in six drafts. The last three were copywriting edits. Do you remember?"

"Yeah." Teresa shrugged. "Everyone was really clear about what they wanted."

Tori chortled. "In the proverbial pig's eye. I've seen meetings like that go into thirty drafts just for the art. You have a special talent, Teresa. Why do you think you're going on this trip?"

"Because I'm available?"

Tori rolled her eyes. "Or you're good at what you do. Oh — there's the boss."

Rayann joined them carrying a large satchel in one hand, her laptop case in the other and a cell phone held between shoulder and ear. "I'm really sorry," she was saying. "I was really looking forward to it, too. I'm getting in a cab now. Uh-huh. When I get back. Probably Sunday. I will want full and complete delivery of my cuddles and kisses upon return. Love to Dee." She set down the computer case and caught the cell phone before it slid to the sidewalk.

Teresa tried to look as if she hadn't heard a word. So there *was* someone in Rayann's life. There hadn't been any clues so far. And why should she care, anyway?

Tori shifted her bags. "What did you have to cancel?"

Rayann sighed. "I was going to babysit my new goddaughter." She pressed the cell phone to her heart. "The new woman in my life."

Teresa chewed her bottom lip. So she was back to square one on understanding anything about Rayann's private life.

"Children do that, don't they?" Tori's expression included Ray in a club that Teresa couldn't yet join. "It doesn't matter what shape your heart is in, they just make themselves at home."

The airport shuttle pulled up. As they piled in, Teresa missed some of what Tori and Rayann were saying. When they were settled, Rayann was admitting, "And already my attitude has been changing about lots of things. Suddenly I feel entitled to have an opinion about schools and curricula. Crime and punishment — that changed overnight. The day after Joyner was born I heard some ghastly news report about this man who had sexually molested several grade-school children. All I could think was . . . kill the bastard. Just kill him. He doesn't deserve to live. And he'll just keep doing it, so kill him now. And I've been opposed to the death penalty all my life. Where did that come from?"

"You weren't thinking in the abstract anymore." Tori folded her hands on her stomach, looking very wise. "Love is always transformational."

"Oh, that is true," Rayann said. Her expression was wistful. "That is very true. 'We'll always have the stars.' "

Tori grinned and rested her hand briefly on Rayann's arm as if in total accord. "I always laugh when he lights the cigarettes at the end. But that movie does cover the way love changes people. Especially the love of a child."

"My favorite Bette is *All About Eve*. Hands down." Rayann fished in her satchel. "Air tickets, here."

"I don't disagree," Tori said. "It's one of my favorite movies of all time."

Teresa tucked her ticket into her backpack. Old movies weren't exactly her specialty. She liked Tori well enough, but felt divided from her by a lifetime of experiences. Rayann, on the other hand, had no trouble establishing a rapport with Tori. Teresa watched the scenery flick by and felt a little out of it. She could have sworn that the trades reported Rayann's age as thirty-nine, but she seemed older than that. Maybe it was forty-nine. But she didn't look *that* old. That would make her twenty years older than Teresa, and that was a big gap. Too big, probably.

What's it to you, she demanded of herself. *Too big of a gap for what? Just shup.*

"I thought that was Donna Reed," Tori was saying.

"She was definitely in *It's a Wonderful Life*. But I'm not sure she was Benny Goodman's girlfriend in the biopic. You could be right though. Lou —" Rayann paused for a moment. "I'll have to look it up."

The flight was uneventful. Fasten your seatbelts, drink your coffee, here's your peanuts, please check in the overhead compartment to make sure you didn't leave any belongings behind and buh-bye. The first thing Teresa noticed was that it was warm in Phoenix. She shrugged out of her jacket. "That's better."

"Warm." Tori inhaled deeply. "I like warm."

"There's our car." Rayann walked briskly down the sidewalk.

A young man who didn't look old enough to drive was holding up a sign that said, "Liman's."

The young man introduced himself as "Steve," then spent several minutes fitting their satchels and briefcases in the small trunk of the car. Teresa noticed with amusement that he kept glancing at Rayann. She had that effect on people. Both sexes. If Rayann noticed she gave no indication, but Steve's tongue was draped over the steering wheel when Rayann got into the seat next to him.

Teresa decided right then and there that she was not going to be a Steve. Yes, she was having some undeniable problems with her own tongue, especially when in unexpected moments she heard something in the timbre of Rayann's voice that reminded her of the alley and the way Rayann had felt against her. But she was not going to be a puppy. Rayann would not respect that — she wouldn't even notice.

What had locked up Rayann's heart that way? Teresa's observation was that some of the light was getting back into Rayann's inner self, but she was still a far cry from the vibrant, passionately alive — okay, and bitchy — woman she had been.

Nothing to do with you, Reese. When you get home you're going to ask Lisa in legal for a date. There's far more chance of some fun and double-backed aardvarking with Lisa than you'll ever have with Rayann Germaine.

"I am really sorry to have to bring you down here." Cindy Degas tapped across the cement floor of the hardware store.

"We want to do the job right, Cindy." Rayann had worked with her before. Cindy was the reason she had managed to swipe this account from one of the big firms. "It's not that unusual to get started with shooting and have major regrets about the entire project. Given that we're new partners, I should have anticipated this problem."

Cindy pushed her lush blonde hair back over her shoulder. "Thanks for not implying we don't know what we want."

Rayann would never imply that to a client, as tempted as she might be. "These are my colleagues, Teresa Mandrell and Tori Raguza. They are the best. Where's Jena keeping herself?"

"In the back." Cindy led the way through the idle cameras and sound equipment that cluttered up half of the store. It was the company's most recently built store and they had insisted on using it in the commercial shoot.

They tromped after Cindy. Rayann muttered to Tori and Teresa, "Cindy and I go back a few years to when she worked for a textiles firm. Step lightly — her spring is coiled really tight."

"Oh, joy." Tori said.

Two actors lounged in chairs, both reading, and representatives from the local technical trade union were drinking coffee and looking sleepy. Rayann could imagine that Cindy was looking at all of them with the sound of a cash register ringing in her head.

Jena looked as if Cindy had been hand-feeding her tacks. She'd been very upset that she'd had to call for back-up. She'd been in advertising long enough to handle a commercial shoot on her own. She glared at the idle crew. "They all go off the clock in five minutes. Union rules. Since we contracted, they're back at nine a.m. whether we need them or not." The tension of the two unsuccessful days working on the shoot showed in her voice. She definitely sounded less Emma Thompson and more Eliza Doolittle.

"Let's need them," Rayann said. She raised her voice. "Actors only — could we just run through the script you have."

The sage-looking older man helped the soccer mom type find a piece of plumbing hardware.

Thirty seconds later Rayann sighed. "Thanks everybody. We'll see you in the morning." She turned to Cindy. "Where can we work?"

"I booked the three of you a big suite that has a large conference table, modem hook-ups, the works. You're on the floor above where Jena and I are."

As they drove back across Phoenix toward the airport hotel area, Rayann found herself squeezed in the back seat with Cindy between her and Teresa. It had seemed preferable to being squished against hormonally challenged Steve. Jena had that honor, with Tori smashed against the window. Cindy was having no problem with the seating arrangement but Rayann was remembering all the times she'd turned down Cindy's overtures. Her reason why — Louisa — didn't exist anymore. But she still had no interest in Cindy. She had no interest in anyone.

The suite was as large as Cindy had promised. Teresa and she took the two bedrooms on the left,

Tori one of the two on the right. The bellman distributed the various satchels as directed, looking a little puzzled at the lack of luggage.

Room service arrived about the same time they settled down to work. Rayann munched on an onion ring and addressed herself to Cindy. "Now, how is it we all approved a commercial that could have been written for your biggest competitor? There wasn't one ounce of differentiation. All it lacked was that football coach guy."

Cindy shook her head. "I've been asking myself that all day."

Jena chimed in. "It's partly the way the actors are delivering. They've seen those ads. So has the director."

"We have to do better." Rayann finished the onion ring and went on to the hamburger. "What are you sketching, Teresa?"

"I'm just making backdrops of the store. And some paper dolls of the actors. It'll save a lot of work."

Teresa reminded Rayann of herself ten years ago. "For this you went to the Sorbonne?"

Teresa chuckled. "This is more fun than copying the *Mona Lisa*. I mean you finish copying the *Mona Lisa* and all you have is proof positive that you're no DaVinci."

Rayann grinned. Teresa did have a tendency to make her smile. Which, she supposed, was good for her.

Cindy nibbled delicately on her toasted cheese sandwich as she leaned over to look at the sketches. Some of her long, blonde wisps draped over Teresa's shoulder. Rayann blinked. Cindy's radar had obviously picked up something she'd missed. Of course Teresa was a lesbian. She'd been crazy to miss it herself. Not that it made any difference. Well, yes it did. It was always great to find out that someone that talented was gay.

"You know where I think we went wrong?" Tori flipped open her laptop and turned it on. "We were so eager to differentiate them from the big warehouse chain that we emphasized personal service and ended up looking just like their other major competitor."

"We want women in the door. And most women won't go into a hardware store unless someone will give them advice on what to buy. And at the same time they're afraid of getting ripped off. All the research suggests that." Cindy swept a nonexistent crumb off of Teresa's sketch. Rayann kept herself from rolling her eyes as Cindy's hand "accidentally" brushed Teresa's.

Tori pushed the male actor's picture away. "Why is our advice giver gray-haired? That's a little stereotypical, don't you think?"

"Yeah, it is," Rayann said. "I don't know why I didn't see that either. I must still be a little rusty."

Jena picked up the photo. "Okay, let's change this guy to a buffed-out hunk. Isn't a hardware store a great place to meet guys?"

Cindy tucked her hair behind her ear. "Let's change him into the FedEx woman in a tool belt. Now you're talking."

Teresa made a sound between a groan and a giggle. "Who picks the actress?"

Cindy laughed in her megawatt sultry way. Rayann felt compelled to say, "Don't go there, you two."

Teresa looked properly chastised, but Cindy was not repentant. "Maybe we should go after the lesbian dollar. We are the leaders of the do-it-yourself movement, after all."

"No way," Jena said. "You girls have Xena. I want my hunk. Hey — Kevin Sorbo in a tool belt. Yummy."

Rayann pointedly addressed herself to Tori, who could at least be counted on to be mature. "We need to shift the copy from helping her find what she's looking for to helping her understand what she's buying and why. We can get in that point about the premium quality of the house brand items."

"God, Rayann. Work, work, work." Cindy slumped in the chair next to Teresa. "Actually, I think we can tone down the grandfatherly advice angle. I think that *is* what's bothering me. Most of our store clerks are well-trained. Nobody else trains like we do. They know their stuff and they come in all shapes and sizes and ages. And we're proud of how many women work in our stores."

Tori was typing like crazy. "Let me work on this for about ten minutes, okay?"

Cindy waved her hand at the entertainment armoire. "The TV can be used as a display monitor. I checked. All we have to do is ask the concierge for the right cable. They said they had everything."

Rayann relaxed and finished her hamburger. "What did we do before all the conveniences of an office could be found everywhere we went?"

"We had lives," Tori muttered.

Cindy spluttered into her soda. "Ain't that the truth."

Teresa tore several sheets out of her sketchpad. "So what does this ungrandfatherly advice-giver look like? You want to use the same actor but make him a little less Grandpa Walton?"

"I have a novel idea." Rayann looked ceilingward for a moment. "I *am* rusty. It's quite obvious. We switch roles. The woman is the professional, the grandfather the one who needs advice."

"Oh, I like that," Cindy said. "I'm going to have to run it by the powers-that-be, but I like that. The warehouse chain does imply that a little in their ads, but we can do better."

"All the research says that many women trust women more readily than men when it comes to subjects they feel they don't know much about. And that's a change. Fifteen years ago it wasn't that way at all." Rayann got out her own laptop. "Let me write up a brief memo you can use with your boss, Cindy. There's valid market research. This is not radical."

The room fell quiet as everyone busily tapped. Cindy went to the phone in one of the bedrooms and ordered up the monitor cable and a miniature inkjet printer.

They finished before ten. Jena cried exhaustion and headed to her room on the floor below. Cindy insisted on taking the rest of them downstairs for drinks.

Tori excused herself after one round. Rayann wanted to excuse herself as well, but something made her stay. Maybe it was the way Cindy so obviously had plans for Teresa's night. Teresa was starting to show signs of resistance, but Cindy didn't hear no as quickly as she heard yes. Rayann wondered if she was just a little piqued that Cindy wasn't flirting with her at all. No. She was just a little worried on Teresa's behalf. She was so young.

Not that young, she amended. But young enough. And attractive enough. She could see why Cindy preferred her. Over the last ten years Rayann had lost her youthful slenderness, and the last year had taken its toll on her face.

Well, that's a new perspective, she thought. She sipped her soda and tried to remember the last time she had felt like the old one in the crowd. A long, long time. Had she aged for Louisa — in the sense of learning more about the things that Louisa liked that had happened before she was born? Definitely. She could talk Big Band with the best of them now.

"Grunge is passé, don't you think?" Teresa put a little air between herself and Cindy. "I used to like entire albums, but lately I feel lucky if I like one or two tracks from some of my favorite bands. Beck, Goo Goo Dolls. Even Green Day. I liked their debuts, but the follow-ups were disappointing."

Rayann had never heard of the bands Teresa mentioned but Cindy was nodding. Cindy couldn't be a year younger than she was. Cindy was also closing up the space Teresa had created.

"I like Tori Amos. And though I blush to admit it, I did like some of the Spice Girls stuff. Do you go to a lot of concerts?"

"No, I just listen to a lot of all-night radio."

"Rayann, you're mistreating this child."

"She's a professional," Rayann said.

"I'm not a child." Teresa's eyebrows had come together.

"I'm just teasing," Cindy said. "You are not a child."

Teresa smiled a little nervously. "Well, this will be my first opportunity for an early night in about two weeks, so if you'll excuse me, I'll turn in."

"One more," Cindy pleaded.

"No thanks. See you in the morning."

Rayann admired the deft way Teresa had escaped. Cindy was watching after her. When she disappeared from view, she sighed.

"Any chance you'll stay another night?"

"Leave her alone, Cindy."

Cindy turned her sharp, eager gaze on Rayann. She scooted across the booth seat until her knees touched Rayann's. "Do I hear a proprietorial tone?"

"She's my employee."

"She's also a free woman, unlike you."

Rayann realized then that there was no way Cindy could know about Louisa. It wasn't as if she'd sent out notices to everyone she had ever met. She swallowed hard. "Louisa died last year."

Cindy's temptress façade melted. "Oh, Rayann, am I so sorry. I didn't know."

"Of course you didn't. She was crossing the street and she was hit by a drunk driver." It was all she could bring herself to say.

"That's awful. Oh, that must have been terrible for you."

"It was hard," she admitted. "Well, Teresa's not the only one who has been burning the midnight oil. I could use a good night's sleep."

"I'll walk you back to your room. Maybe I can change Teresa's mind." Cindy the temptress was back.

"Give it up, Cindy. You struck out." She started to sidle out of the booth but Cindy caught her hand.

"I'm beginning to think that you have hang-ups about sex."

"Why, because I never went to bed with you?" Cindy's hand was warm. It was real flesh and blood.

"Partly. And you seem so gung-ho to keep Teresa

out of bed, too. It used to be that being gay was about being sex-positive. As in there's nothing wrong with two happy adults having fun together."

"I'm too tired to debate the politics of sexual liberation with you. Not tonight. It takes two to foxtrot." She pulled her hand away from Cindy's grasp and cursed herself for missing the warmth of it.

"I understand that. But what's the deal with monogamy? I don't want to be callous, but what's stopping you now?"

Rayann's anger made her see white. "That is a callous question, but I'll tell you. I gave her my word. I gave her my vow. I gave her my love. And she was all I could ever have wanted. And I still love her."

"You love the memory of her."

"You are an incredible bitch, Cindy."

Cindy shrugged. "So I've been told." Her expression softened. "I'm sorry. I was just pissed. Teresa's very nice, but she's not you. I wasted all night when I have the feeling..." She put her hand on Rayann's shoulder. "I have the feeling that with a little persistence, I might discover a new volcano."

Her body was crying out for intimacy. She couldn't deny it. Cindy had no idea just how sex positive Rayann could be. But not tonight. "See me in a year." Her tone was not as light as she had hoped it would be.

"Who are you? Queen Victoria?" Cindy's fingertips brushed her ear.

"You're being callous again."

"Your heart is racing."

"It does that."

"Don't cheat yourself." Her other hand snaked over Rayann's thigh.

Suddenly Cindy was too close. There was no air. She snapped, "The answer is no, Cindy. Don't act like a guy, okay?"

Cindy sat back. "Well, that's pretty final. Two San Francisco lesbians in my lap and I'm going to bed alone. Who would have thought it?"

"Goodnight, Cindy." She slid out of the booth.

Cindy tossed off the last of her drink. "Sweet dreams."

Her dreams weren't sweet, they were nonexistent. Somewhere around three, Rayann roused herself and went out to the main room of the suite to forage for milk in the mini-bar. She drained the pint and stood looking at the twinkling lights.

She didn't know when she started to cry. Maybe she'd been crying all along and there had been no tears. She cried because she was faithless, because a quick tumble in bed with Cindy had tempted her. What kind of lover had she been? How could Louisa do this to her?

She heard movement behind her. Startled, she turned on the tall T-shirt-clad form.

"I couldn't sleep. And then I thought you might need . . . help." Teresa was all concern and earnestness. Rayann felt a million years older.

"I'm sorry I woke you."

"No, I just couldn't sleep. Strange room, I guess. Will you be okay?"

Rayann wiped her eyes. Once they'd begun, the tears wouldn't stop. Just as she had so many months ago to Teddy, she said, "No."

She didn't know how it happened, but her head was on Teresa's shoulder. It was inappropriate. It was weak. She found a small measure of control and gently pushed Teresa away.

"Do you want to talk about it?"

She shook her head. "It'll pass."

She sensed Teresa was holding herself back and she mentally thanked her for the restraint. Another word and she would start to cry again.

"I have a confession to make," Teresa said, unexpectedly. She looked up inquiringly. "We had met before. Before the elevator, I mean."

She managed a word around the boulder in her throat. "Really?"

"Yeah. Do you remember a prissy little insecure employee at your old company? Who quit in the middle of a meeting?"

Rayann racked her brain. What was she talking about? She searched Teresa's expression, but the light was too dim to read any meaning. "I'm sorry, I don't."

"I thought so. Well, that was me."

"When was this?"

"Early last summer. I was just out of school."

"Oh. I wasn't myself. It was probably my fault."

Teresa looked as if she could say more on the subject, but she didn't. "Is it the same problem now?"

She nodded. So much time had passed and she seemed so far from the acceptance stage Judy's grief book promised. She'd never get there.

"I'm sorry," Teresa whispered. "Whatever it is . . . I'm sorry."

"Thank you." Teresa got up, all long legs and curves. Inappropriate, Rayann reminded herself. What was wrong with her? "I appreciate that."

"See you in the morning."

Morning wasn't long off. She opened the sliding glass door onto the minuscule balcony. The cool night air felt wonderful on her hot cheeks.

"Rayann? Don't." Teresa was right behind her.

"Don't what?" Comprehension dawned. "I am not going to fucking kill myself. If I was going to do that I'd have done it months ago."

"Sorry," Teresa snapped. "What am I supposed to think?"

"Leave me alone, just leave me alone."

"Fuck you. I just want to help." Teresa spun on her heel and stalked away.

"It was *you*." Rayann grasped the door as her knees wobbled. The face had never registered, but the voice and words had.

Teresa slowly turned back. "What do you mean?"

"In that bar. In the alley behind the bar. What are you, some sort of stalker?"

The silence stretched out until Teresa stepped closer. "It was me." Rayann could see that her lips were trembling. "I saw you go into the bar and curiosity got the better of me. I wondered what on earth the woman who had treated me like pond slime was doing in a gay bar."

"Getting drunk. A fact which you took advantage of."

"Oh, don't go pure and virginal on me. You were the one who didn't want to stop."

They'd gone over a line that set alarms ringing in Rayann's head. "We have to forget it happened."

Teresa's eyes were like reflecting pools. They shimmered in the low light and Rayann could see herself, a tousle of hair and tears. "You go ahead and forget. I never will."

The memory replayed itself on Rayann's body, but this time she wasn't drunk. Hunger consumed her — she needed to be held, touched, loved.

Teresa's mouth was suddenly on hers, capturing her tiny whimper. She was fierce, then tender, then breathing hard into Rayann's ear. "I'm sorry."

Her hands found their way under Teresa's T-shirt. "This is wrong."

She moved Rayann's hands from her back to her ribs. "If you say so. To me it's unfinished business."

Her thumbs brushed Teresa's nipples, wrenching a moan from her. "We're going to wake up the others. We can't."

For an answer, Teresa drew her toward the closest bedroom, which was Rayann's. Once the door was closed she peeled off her T-shirt. Rayann swallowed hard. Her mouth was dry. She couldn't think.

Teresa pressed her down onto the bed, then offered her bare breasts to Rayann's mouth with a quiet, "Put me out of my misery."

The floodgates were opened. Tears and passion coated Rayann's mouth and fingers. Stretched out on the bed they were breast to breast. Rayann strained against the past and found Teresa's quiet need as compelling and arousing as any of her life. She remembered how Louisa had felt against her — it was impossible not to. It was impossible not to feel guilty, impossible not to love every moment. Impossible not to want to do it again, impossible not to hear the echo of Louisa's cries when Teresa trembled against her.

Rayann could not have said how long their drive to mutual release and satisfaction lasted. It seemed to take forever to get there and it was over too soon.

When the throb of her heartbeat subsided, all she heard was Teresa crying. "Don't," she whispered. "Please don't."

"I'm sorry."

"I'm not." It was true. Guilt was consuming her now that the hunger was gone. But she wasn't sorry.

"You must think me such a fool."

The sun was coming up and the soft light outlined the womanly curves of Teresa's shoulders and hips. "No. I think you're beautiful."

There was a bruised expression on Teresa's face. "I didn't necessarily want this to happen."

"I know," Rayann assured her. "Neither did I."

It was time for her to suggest that they put it behind them. It was just one of those things, she should say.

Teresa put her hand on Rayann's bare thigh. Her mouth looked swollen as it closed around Rayann's nipple.

Rayann found herself urging Teresa's fingers inside her.

Then Teresa's mouth was at her ear. "But I want to do this."

I want you to, Rayann thought. She was beyond words. She let her body say it. She let her body say it over and over.

Drained and exhausted, Teresa slipped into her own room. Just one of those things, she had agreed while Rayann's hands teased her breasts. They would put it behind them. She'd agreed to that, too, as she kissed the length of Rayann's spine. Continuing was inappropriate, she had murmured, her fingers deep inside Rayann where she so obviously needed them. They couldn't repeat it, absolutely not.

She curled up in the darkness and touched her fingertips to her lying mouth.

11

Teresa was awakened by Tori's pounding on the door. "Breakfast is here! We have to get moving soon."

She slipped into the shower, then dressed. Finally, when she could avoid it no longer, she looked at herself in the mirror.

She looked just the same. She peered at the wrinkle. Considering what had happened, she would have thought it would at least be different.

What she had experienced with Rayann just didn't show. She'd had sex before, but never with such emotional engagement. She had lost herself in

Rayann's body, drowned in Rayann's passion. She had felt whatever pain it was that stabbed at Rayann and not understood it. She wanted to make the pain go away.

Which was not, all in all, a good foundation for a relationship. Did she want a relationship with Rayann? Yes. But what was a relationship? Living together? Marriage? A trip to the movies once in a while?

How did you get to be twenty-eight and not know the answer? She made a face at herself.

"Come on, Teresa! You want coffee or tea?"

She went out to the dining cart, her gaze focused on the food. She heard Rayann's voice in her bedroom and relaxed. The inevitable morning-after embarrassment was postponed.

She drank all of the orange juice, gobbled the toast and started in on the eggs. The phone in Tori's room rang and she hurried to answer it, leaving Teresa alone. She strained to distinguish Rayann's muted words. She sounded distressed.

You are *not* responsible for her state of mind, she told herself sharply, but her body wasn't listening. She casually moved toward the painting that hung next to Rayann's door. It was one of those imaginary landscapes, all ferns and grottos.

"Why do I feel this way?" Rayann sounded on the edge of tears. "Well, how should I feel? Christ, Judy, as a friend you can be worthless sometimes." She listened for a few moments. "I know. I know. I let it happen. And I am so . . . ashamed. The guilt is killing me."

Tori was coming out of her bedroom, so Teresa managed a nonchalant stroll back to the dining cart.

Her mind was churning. Ashamed? Guilty? It had been glorious, and Rayann Germaine was ashamed of it? Ashamed of what? Of wanting someone? Of having needs?

"You look tired." Tori was rifling through the jelly packets.

"I didn't sleep well."

"Rayann said the same thing. I slept like a baby, though. I need a new bed."

Teresa choked down a forkful of eggs. When Rayann finally came out of her room she could not look up.

"Good morning, Teresa. Is there any coffee left?" She sounded hatefully cool and composed.

"I think so," she managed to answer. She handed the carafe to Rayann without actually meeting her gaze. Rayann sounded as if she was having no trouble putting it all behind her, even the shame and the guilt of really great sex. Teresa felt consumed by the old anger. If she wanted to be honest with herself, she'd gotten so angry the first time Rayann criticized her because she had had a bad case of hero worship. She had thought she would learn from Rayann and turn into another successful lesbian in advertising. Instead, she'd found out her idol had a bad temper and the ability to skewer just about anybody.

Well, Rayann was not her idol anymore. She was not someone to be looked up to, not in the least.

Damn, Teresa thought. Not an idol, just human. A woman with weaknesses mixed in with strengths. You can't love an idol, she told herself.

Crap.

Once again Rayann was putting her in uncharted

territory. The creepy butterfly feeling was back. She had no idea what to do next. She had never been in love before.

The actors were professionals. They learned their new lines quickly and had no trouble adapting to the changed roles. The director seemed much more awake to Teresa and it was clear that the shoot was going to go smoothly. Jena no longer looked suicidal and Cindy was joking with everyone.

You could have had sex with Cindy, she reminded herself. But no, you had to get in bed with the boss's boss. That was not smart. Another in a long line of stupid moves.

The stupidity of it became even more apparent over the next week. She was aware of Rayann at every moment. It was as if she'd developed a Rayann sonar. She knew when Rayann was on the phone, when she was walking by, where she was headed. She could sense when she was angry or sad or tense or frustrated.

She never sensed happy. She never sensed that Rayann paused near her cubicle and wondered, just a little, how Teresa was doing.

Like the entire history of their nonexistent relationship, Rayann was pretending that Teresa the person didn't exist.

What did she want from Rayann? She had asked herself that so many times she didn't know the answer anymore. She wanted to understand her. She'd found Rayann's picture in her backpack and couldn't help but study it. She wanted to know what it was that had sucked all the joy out of her, but left her with such a capacity for passion.

Rayann had plenty of uses for Teresa the artist, though. It seemed that Jim Dettman only assigned her to projects that involved working directly with Rayann, including an endless stream of brainstorming sessions for new clients and old, and even a sketch of a C.E.O. for a company's annual report.

Rayann was walking toward her now. Every muffled tread on the thick carpet was like an explosion to Teresa.

"Have a minute? I've got good news and a request for some of your scarce leisure time for a worthy cause."

"Sure," Teresa said.

"How about my office?"

She knew the moment the door was closed. They were alone and it felt as if the room was electrically charged.

"The good news is that Philip approved quarterly bonuses this morning. And you are going to get one. Congratulations."

She managed a quick flick of eye contact. "Any particular reason?"

"How about working like a dog? You've put in really long hours and you've been very productive." Rayann's voice was a little hoarse, as if she had a cold. "I think actually you're working too hard. So I have a gift of a couple of days off with the condition that you use them right away. Also, Philip agrees that you should be moved up to the next salary grade. You may not have been in advertising very long, but your work — especially in groups — is that of someone with a great deal of experience."

"I learned a lot from my boss at the museum. She was good with people."

There was a short silence, then Rayann said, "I'd like to get your help with a pro bono project, if you're interested."

"What kind?"

"It's for the Tenderloin Housing Agency. They want to raise money for a commercial garden that is otherwise going to be turned into a parking lot by day and a junkie hangout by night."

"A community garden, right in the middle of the city? That's going to be some expensive corn."

"The land has a toxics problem that won't clear it for residential use. But it can grow flowers. They have a local nursery willing to provide the organic know-how, and I think we can get our wholesale nursery client to kick in the first year's plants. What they need is something I thought you would really enjoy — a mural for the building walls alongside the garden. They have all the eager young painters lined up and all the supplies have been donated. But they don't have a design."

Teresa forgot she wasn't looking at Rayann. "That sounds really interesting. Will I need to submit a design for approval?"

"Yes, but they have no real concept in mind. However, they specifically want to avoid anything political. They'd love to underscore the purpose of the garden."

Teresa was rapidly considering ideas. "Where's the location?"

Rayann gave her a slip of paper. "Address and the name of my contact at THA. I'm glad you'll do it." Rayann's gaze lingered and Teresa felt herself flushing.

She dropped her gaze to Rayann's desk. "What happened?" She indicated a long scratch.

"Henry dropped a VCR. The desk survived, the VCR didn't. He was trying to lift too much." She ran her finger in the groove. "It can be repaired."

"Well." Teresa glanced at the paper. "Thanks for this. And the bonus and the raise. My cup runneth over."

"You earned it, Teresa." She was at the door when Rayann said huskily, "Teresa."

She loved the way her name sounded when Rayann said it, but she couldn't turn around. "Yes?"

"Look at me."

She slowly turned and her gaze was pulled into the well of Rayann's eyes.

"I just want you to know that you really earned it. The money, it . . . it has nothing to do with what happened."

"I never thought it did. I don't believe you're that kind of person." Rayann would not pay someone off to keep an embarrassing secret.

"And I didn't think you would need incentives to — to forget about it." Rayann closed her eyes as if that was the only way to break their eye contact. "It sounds so sordid, put that way."

There was nothing sordid about it, Teresa wanted to say. "I never said I'd forget about it," she whispered and she made her escape before Rayann could say anything more.

What had she done? For the thousandth time, Rayann wondered how she could undo the distress she had obviously caused Teresa. It had been wrong to unload first her grief then all her pent-up physical needs on someone so young, so obviously inexperienced. Well, she wasn't inexperienced at sex, but life was another thing. She seemed so . . . unsuspecting.

She ran her finger into the groove left by the VCR. The desk had a thick veneer of cherry over pine. The pine that showed could be stained to match the cherry.

"I got your tools." Henry hovered at the door. "That place was neat."

She took the leather roll from him. She'd had all of her chisels sharpened. Since Joyner's birth, an idea for a window hanging for Joyner's room had been buzzing around in her head.

"I'm real sorry about that." Henry rubbed the groove as if that would make it go away.

"Don't be." Rayann had a sudden impulse. "In fact, it can be the first part of a new artwork." She unrolled the coiled pouches and selected a grooving tool. "It could be the branch of a tree or the arch of a vine." She smoothed the groove, then selected a smaller tool. A familiar and long-absent calm settled on her as a many-fingered leaf sprouted from the original groove.

It was hours before she wearied of bending over the desk. The office had in fact gone quiet. No one was working late on such a beautiful evening, apparently. She looked out the window in disbelief at what was left of a searing red sunset. A quarter of her desktop was covered in twining vines and leaves, the sharp white of the pine showing through the cherry in vivid contrast. Washed with a brown-green dye and filled with veneer it would be gorgeous. Of course, Phil wasn't paying her to decorate desks.

She rolled up her tools and confronted a wave of sadness. *You're really gone, aren't you, Lou? I'm moving on.*

Acceptance. She felt a wrench of loss and realized how she had clung to the pain as a way of keeping her distance from life.

"You should just put up a sign."

Rayann jumped. Teresa was framed in the doorway. "What?"

"A sign. A great big one with full disclosure."

Rayann was certain she did not want to have this conversation with Teresa. Teresa was obviously upset, but Rayann couldn't fathom why. "We probably shouldn't do this."

"It would say, 'Dear World. Whatever you do, don't care for me. Don't help me. I am in too much pain. I'm the only person in the world who can understand my pain, so don't ask.' "

"What do you know about pain?" Stop, she told herself. This was pointless.

"Nothing, obviously. I'm just a babe in the wood. I don't have the capacity to understand human suffering."

"You've never lost anyone you loved."

"How do you know?"

Rayann arched an eyebrow. "It would be etched in your face the way it's etched in mine."

"You mean carved." Teresa waved a hand at the desk. Tears glistened in her eyes. "Just like this. Meticulously crafted and carved. Lovingly slaved over. You made yourself a monument to pain."

"You don't know anything about it," Rayann snapped hoarsely.

"That's right. Because you won't tell me."

Anger and reason were at war inside her. Reason dictated that she should not unburden herself on Teresa. It would only draw them closer, and closer was not something they could ever be. Never. There was only Louisa.

But anger won. She picked up Louisa's picture and ran her fingertips over that beautiful face. "She died. She got hit by a truck and spent three and a half months in intensive care. And then she died."

"My mother died when I was two. I don't even remember her."

Rayann gripped the frame so hard her knuckles turned white. "She was *not* my mother. She was my *lover*. For ten years." She gasped for breath, but anger had the upper hand. "She was the finest woman I have known, that I ever will know. She was the best part of me. She suffered. Horribly. And they gave me money. As if that makes a difference." She was trembling so hard she had to put the frame down. "She was an incredible lover. She knew all types of literature. She loved old movies. And her son and her grandson. And she loved me." She dashed tears from her eyes. "So forgive me for being in pain. You can't even begin to understand. If I live another hundred years I'll never meet anyone remotely like her — and neither will you." The anger drained out of her when she finally registered Teresa's pale, tear-streaked face. "I'm sorry."

"I asked," Teresa whispered. During her flash of anger, Rayann had been the same woman Teresa had first met. Now she understood why Rayann had seemed like an unfeeling machine. "Thank you for telling me. I want to . . . I want to take the days off you gave me. I came to thank you for them. I cleared it with Jim."

Rayann would have given anything to take the stricken look from Teresa's eyes. She got up, started toward her. "Teresa, I —"

"No. No." Teresa shook her head violently. "No." She dashed out the door.

"Oh shit." She was incredibly weary. She felt as if she'd just walked from San Francisco to New York and back. Keeping all of that anguish bottled up — no wonder she was tired all the time.

Teresa, she thought. Teresa hadn't deserved the things she'd said. How could she call back the words and put the smile back in Teresa's eyes?

"You want one of my Manhattans?" Jill swiped the bar and put down a cocktail napkin.

"Sure," Teresa said. She hadn't come here for the drink, but to talk to Jill. It was late and a weeknight, so Jill might have time to talk. She just wanted some information.

She should have recognized the picture on Rayann's desk as the one that had been enlarged and wreathed at the memorial she and Vivian had walked in on. It would have saved her some mistakes. She might have been able to hold something back.

"One Manhattan. You want to run a tab?"

"No, I'll settle up now." She put a five on the bar. "Can I ask you a question?"

"Sure. It's slow and as everyone knows, I love to talk."

Teresa grinned. "About six months ago, I don't know, maybe longer, I was in here and you were having a memorial or wake. Who was the woman who died? Because I saw her picture recently and remembered. I hate mysteries."

Jill's expression softened. "Oh, that was Louisa Thatcher. A great friend, really. She was one of those people you could count on. She made you want to be better than you were. She owned a bookstore, too. Rare editions and popular stuff. She and her lover added a lesbian section."

A woman of intelligence and character. It made sense. What other kind of woman would someone like Rayann love? Teresa sipped the drink. "That is good, thanks."

"Told you. Friends like Louisa come once in a lifetime. We were all devastated by her being hurt like that, then lingering for so long. If sheer will could grow a bunch of new organs, she would have recovered. I don't know how her lover survived it. It was awful. And I miss Lou so much. Every time you talked to her you felt like she had added something."

"She sounds as if she was really loved."

"Oh yeah. Her son was devoted and Ray — her partner — was really in love. There was a big gap in their ages, but it didn't matter. They clicked. What they didn't share they paid less attention to. What they had in common they really worked at. It was a great thing to see. It made me think about things a little differently. She was quite a woman. They named the women's center in Oakland after her."

Teresa felt like crying. Again. She could never hope to compete with Louisa. She could never replace

Louisa in Rayann's heart. Ten years of loving a woman who could inspire such devotion and loyalty — if Teresa held Rayann up to the light, she would see Louisa indelibly there. So what was there left to hope for?

She thanked Jill for the drink and for satisfying her curiosity. She wandered into a movie but didn't follow much beyond the car crashes, train wrecks and exploding buildings, all of which was just a little too close to reality.

As she walked into the surprisingly mild early spring night she knew there was only one person she could really talk to about how she felt. Vivian was useless when it came to love. She was disgustingly happy and talked about nothing but Kim. She'd said last night that she was considering moving in with Kim when Kim's roommate moved out in a few months. Teresa hoped she would. She'd keep the apartment — no more roommates.

It would be easy to get a flight in the morning after she met with the community garden people. She had the days off and L.A. was just an hour away by plane.

"You don't expect your old man to believe that you got on a plane and dropped in because everything is hunky-dory?"

Teresa crossed her legs, sinking into her favorite old chair. The comforts of home were soothing — though at her age why she should consider her father's house her home was baffling. "I'm sorry I didn't give you much notice." Melanie had insisted the surprise guest was no problem and they'd all gone out to dinner.

"Don't worry about that. Spill the beans."

Melanie had gone to bed, having understood without a word that Teresa wanted to talk to her dad alone.

"Well, I think I'm in love."

"You say that like a death sentence, punkin."

"It feels like it."

Her father's expression tightened. "It's not supposed to. Is the object of your affection unavailable?"

"Oh, she's single, all right. But she's still taken. I've fallen for a single married woman." It was a bad joke, and her father was not fooled.

"You're not making much sense. She's in love with someone else?"

"Most definitely. How long after Mom died did you think you could love someone else the same way again?"

"Oh, I see. Well, it was a long time."

"How long?" She had to know.

"I don't know. No one came along I was interested in. I know that I was lonely pretty quickly. I missed your mom and I missed women." He paused uncomfortably. "I'm sure you don't want to hear about your old dad's sex life."

"I know you weren't a monk."

"I wasn't cut out for it."

"Did you feel guilty? The first time you were with somebody after Mom died?"

Her questions were making him squirm at little, she could tell. But he was the only person she could ask. "Yes. I felt very guilty. I felt as if I'd cheated on her. It was just something I had to get over."

"How long did that take?"

"A year. A little more than that. I guess I should be specific. I no longer felt guilty about having desires. I'm a body as well as a mind. But I still felt guilty when I enjoyed another woman's laugh, the way she smelled — things that I had loved about your mother. And that took a few more years."

Teresa sniffed. "Great. I'll be thirty-five before she might be ready to love me."

"Who is this vestal virgin?"

Teresa had to smile, albeit wanly. "My boss's boss."

"Reese."

"I know. It's pretty stupid, isn't it? I finally get around to falling in love and it's not just doomed from the get go, but what the working world calls inappropriate."

"It's not doomed — you just might have to be patient."

"The woman who died, she was some sort of paragon. They named a whole women's center after her." She'd found the Thatcher Center's web page through Yahoo and read the short bio of the sainted Louisa Thatcher. She hadn't been rich or particularly famous, oh no, just an ordinary woman with strong ideals and an unshakable belief in building communities. She apparently inspired everyone who ever met her. "I can't compete with that."

"Are you sure she wants you to?"

"I don't know what she wants. I know that she feels something for me, but I'm not sure it's more than just a primitive lust. I don't want to be her

211

getting-over-it toy." She swabbed at her eyes with her sleeve.

"You can't be the person she lost, punkin. Don't try. If she's going to care for you it has to be for who you are. And maybe your not reminding her too much of who she lost is a good thing."

Teresa brightened a little. She hadn't thought of it that way. "You think?"

"Don't get all starry-eyed. I'm not going to give you good odds. If it's been less than a year, you can't trust anything she feels. It's all upside down."

Back to glum. "Thanks, Dad."

"Sorry I couldn't be all roses and valentines." He patted her hand.

"I didn't want you to be. I appreciate it."

"Want some hot chocolate?"

She nodded and went with him to the kitchen. He gave her the oversized mug she'd used since she was a child. It felt good to be home but at the same time she felt like a guest. Nothing stayed the same.

She settled into what had once been her bed and considered what her father had told her.

The future did not look good.

Melanie made great waffles, but Teresa had learned that at Christmas. Her father had devoured two enormous ones with blueberry jam and departed for his Saturday morning round of golf.

"I couldn't possibly eat another one," Teresa told her.

"I'm sure you couldn't." Melanie put the waffle on

Teresa's plate anyway. It steamed, "Eat me," at her. She slathered it with butter and syrup.

"How's your job?" Melanie sat down with her own waffle and sipped her coffee.

Teresa got a shock. In the bright morning light, and without makeup on, Melanie looked a good deal younger than Teresa had supposed. "I love it. It's great. I am functioning as an artist, not just a computer jockey. It feels really good."

"Your dad always says you're a great artist. I like that sketch you did of him."

"Well, that's my dad." She managed a large forkful of waffle. Her stomach felt as if it would burst, but it was so good.

Melanie chuckled. "Yeah, he says I look like Meryl Streep."

"You do, a little. It's the nose."

Melanie was obviously pleased.

"Can I ask you a question?"

"Sure."

"How old are you?"

"Forty-five in May."

"Oh." Teresa didn't mean to sound so surprised.

"You thought I was older, didn't you?"

"Well . . ." Teresa didn't want to say that Melanie had *looked* older. Vivian would kill her for that kind of rudeness. "I figured since Ken was my age, that you were at least fifty."

Melanie made a face at her coffee. "I had Ken, unwed, when I was sixteen. I never married Ken's father though he had a very active role in raising Ken. We went through a really rough time when he gave up Flower Power and got religion. He married this self-righteous b —" She bit back what she'd been going to say.

"Go right ahead," Teresa said. "I can swear with the best of them."

"Self-righteous bitch. First thing she does is impress upon my happy six-year-old darling Ken that he's illegitimate and will have to work that much harder to get into heaven. I nearly ripped her hair out of her thoughtless little head. Ken is still trying to get over that image."

Teresa thought that explained a lot about Ken. She realized she'd eaten half of the waffle. Her stomach ached. She put down the fork.

"Anyway," Melanie went on, "I was a single mom. My folks helped me get my real estate license and I got by. I dated but never got serious about anybody. I think I was waiting for your dad."

There was a flash of something in Melanie's eyes that Teresa had seen at the wedding, but had not recognized. Now she knew what it was — love. "I tried to raise him right," Teresa said.

"You did good. It never seems like he's ten years older than I am."

Rayann was ten years older than she was, and it seemed like an eternity, Teresa thought. She felt as if she had more in common with Melanie. "I would have never guessed you were. You two are made for each other."

"It's not surprising you didn't realize. My makeup adds years."

"I thought it was supposed to take them off."

Melanie's expression was wry. "My skin is incredibly sensitive to sunlight. My foundation is a little on the thick side — I think it makes me look like a smoker, know what I mean?"

Teresa nodded. "So you can't use any of that magic anti-wrinkle cream? Every time I go into Nordstrom they want to spackle me with it."

"Be careful," Melanie said. "Once you start you won't want to stop."

"Yeah — first one's free."

Melanie laughed. She pushed her plate away. "That's enough of that."

"They're delicious, but I can't finish this one."

"Don't worry, my feelings are not hurt." Melanie stirred her coffee and sipped. She said, a little too nonchalantly, "Your dad said you were having a problem with an affair of the heart. I don't have a lot of experience, but if there's anything I can do . . ."

Teresa was touched. She could not think of Melanie as a mother, but she could certainly use an older sister. Or just a friend. "Well, I'm in love with a woman who is still in love with her dead partner."

"That's not easy," Melanie said.

"No, it's not."

"Are you sure it's love?"

Teresa was surprised by the question. She had never doubted it. "I think so. I mean, I've thought I was in love before. But it always seemed to fizzle. I'd build up this image of the object of my affection and somehow they'd always manage not to fit it anymore. I was completely infatuated with a classmate in France until I discovered she didn't change her underwear every day."

"Gross," Melanie said emphatically.

"That's what I thought," Teresa said. "The gilding

rubbed right off that lily. But the woman I'm in love with — her name is Rayann — I already know her bad side. It doesn't matter. I figure if I think I'm in love when I know how human she can be then I'll still be in love when her good side really blossoms again." It had already started to show at times.

"Maybe it'll work out," Melanie said. "Just don't put your life on hold."

"I'm going to try not to do that."

"In the meantime," Melanie said, "Nine West is having a shoe sale. Interested?"

Teresa perked up. "I don't get any time to shop when I'm at home. It's all I can do to keep up with the laundry and bills. Okay, sometimes I shop because I haven't done the laundry, but that's necessity, not fun." Teresa helped Melanie clear away the breakfast dishes.

Her father complained of neglect when she and Mel returned in the afternoon, laden with bags and shoe boxes. Teresa felt lighter in heart than she would have thought possible. She had a life to get on with. Maybe Rayann would be in it, maybe not. She felt she had achieved equanimity until she woke up in a sweat and could have sworn that she could smell Rayann on her hands and face.

12

Joyner sucked happily on the tip of Rayann's little finger. Her tiny eyes were closed and Rayann resisted the urge to take her finger away so they would open again. Judy had said that the primary rule of parenting was Never Wake a Sleeping Baby.

"What do you want from this, Ray?" Judy was busy with the breast pump. She had not appreciated Rayann's mooing sounds.

"I don't know. I mean, I hardly know her. She's young, what's there to know?"

"Good thing Louisa didn't think that way." Judy

winced as the suction began. "I am amazed by women who breastfeed for a year or even two years. I want this over as soon as possible. Six months tops."

It did not look like fun. "I'm sorry — she's not a lightweight. But she's short on life experiences. Compared to Louisa, I mean."

"Well, that's hardly fair. Louisas are not exactly walking around all over the place. She was really special. Don't think I haven't put myself in your shoes." Judy settled back and took a long swig from her water bottle. "Given Dee's profession, I've imagined losing her. I've wondered what I would do."

"I did that. I accepted that Louisa would die before me — she was almost thirty years older. I just wasn't ready. And we had plans. I was going to make a bundle of dough and eventually we'd sell the bookstore and travel while Louisa was still young enough to climb the Eiffel Tower and walk the Great Wall of China." She sighed wistfully. "Then it was all gone."

"Dee and I have plans. Now they include waiting until Joyner is on her own before we get to some of them. Dee will be close to retirement then. But if something happened to her, the last thing I'd do was go looking for another Dee to take her place. Do you see what I mean?"

"There isn't another Dee. There isn't another Louisa."

Judy fluttered her eyelashes. "Occasionally, I do know something."

Joyner had stopped sucking. Rayann gently removed her pruney finger and settled Joyner on her lap. She looked adorable in the bunny sleeper Rayann had bought her for Easter. "So I shouldn't expect Teresa to be Louisa. But really, I hardly know her. I know what she's like to work with. She's funny and really intuitive. And she's thoughtful and vocal — she's not afraid to talk." Rayann lost her train of thought as she remembered Teresa's frantically whispered demands when they had made love. Teresa was certainly not afraid to say what she wanted.

"So when are you getting married?"

"Judy! That's not what I meant."

"Don't wake up the peanut." Judy switched the pump to her other breast. "You're acting as if you have to decide right now, today, whether a woman you feel a physical attraction to is going to replace Louisa in your life."

"I hurt her. I think she wants to be more than just a romp in the hay."

"If that's going to happen, it'll happen. Just give it time. You got your condo keys today — you know what a drain moving is. Don't rush into anything."

"Why were you never this full of advice before? You were always giving me the party line about not giving quickie answers to friends who needed professional help."

Judy's smile was benign. "You're not talking to a therapist anymore. You're talking to a mom."

"No one is ever going to replace Louisa."

"Of course not. Not ever. You gave Louisa your whole heart. You're going to have to grow new places for new people to take root in you. Okay, that was a therapist talking. Maybe I should charge you."

"I'll swap you babysitting." She looked down into

Joyner's round face. Her entire body was devoted to sleeping. "If I could sleep like that I'd have the energy of twenty women. Moving would be a snap."

"Now that she's here I do sleep like that. I don't have a choice."

"Well, toddle off to bed. If she wakes up I'll feed her and keep her happy until Dee gets home."

"Use the bottle I just filled. It can sit out for six hours without developing any bacteria. Thanks for the sleep." Judy paused long enough to gently kiss the little fist that had escaped the blanket.

When Joyner stirred a half-hour later, Rayann rocked slowly and succeeded in putting her back to sleep. If only the world was this simple. Oh, Joyner, she thought. Love sucks. Stay this age forever. So what if you're toothless and incontinent? Someone else does all the work.

There had been times when she would have given Joyner the advice to never fall in love. The pain was just not worth it. She seemed so fragile. Rayann wanted to protect her from all the bad in the world. Months of grieving had made her accept that you couldn't survive the bad without love, even if love hurt.

How had Teresa gotten involved in this mess? What did she want from Teresa? What did she have to give Teresa in return?

She was not ready to rush into anything. Judy — damn her — was right. She had given her whole heart to Louisa and there was nothing left for Teresa. At least not right now. Tomorrow she would start a new pattern of life, in a new home where Louisa had never set foot. The house in Oakland hadn't sold yet, so she was leaving almost all of the furniture there until it did. Her new home was going to be bare bones, making it even harder to feel as if it *was* home. She needed to guard against filling its emptiness with Teresa. Teresa deserved better.

But as inappropriate as it was, she did not want to end things either. Being around Teresa made her feel more alive. It was as if Teresa possessed some magic spell that dispelled darkness and made ordinary light shimmer with rainbows.

She really didn't know anything about her. Not her favorite movie, not her favorite artists. What if Teresa was one of those women who thought magazines were books? Did she like Virginia Woolf? Had she read any Henry James? Did she think that the movie *Beloved* lived up to the book?

She relived those incredible hours in bed with Teresa. Louisa had been an amazing lover, the first lover to ever make Rayann understand what sweet surrender meant. She had given over complete control to Louisa, willingly. There had been no such need with Teresa, and therefore it had all felt different. Louisa had rarely needed to take. Teresa needed it and could say so. At no time had she been in any danger of thinking it was Louisa making love to her.

What did she want from Teresa? What did she have to give in return? She rocked and her thoughts turned in circles.

It was late when Dedric got home and by all rights, Rayann should have headed back to Oakland for as much sleep as possible. Instead, she drove to what would be her new home and parked in the underground garage. It felt odd. She was not willing to call it excitement yet.

She let herself into the empty living room and

waited a moment to get her bearings in the dark. She opened the curtains that blocked the view from the balcony and looked around her. Once her furniture came it would seem more like hers. But it wouldn't be the same. There would be no stack of thirty or so books waiting to be read, no half-done *New York Times* crossword on the kitchen counter. All the little things that would have made it Louisa's home would not be there. She would have to fill the space by herself.

She stepped onto the balcony. The wind off the bay was sharp and cold, making the night skyline glitter. *If you're looking for me, I'm here.* Images of Teresa intruded and Rayann could not shake them away. Thinking of them both at the same time brought a sharp pang of guilt on both their behalves.

The status quo was intolerable, but Teresa got through it every day. She found a core of what she supposed was professionalism that let her smile, talk and even joke with Rayann while every nerve in her body cried out for something more.

It was pointless. It was all just wasted energy.

When a meeting broke up, she heard Jim Dettman ask Rayann what she looked so happy about. Teresa had noticed it, too. Rayann was finally shining with light on the inside.

"My broker says we have an offer on the house in Oakland. It looks like it should sail through and I won't have to live in two places anymore."

"We had to do that once," Jim said. "We couldn't move all our stuff from the old house because the broker told us empty houses don't sell."

"Exactly. It's been a while since I used packing crates for tables. But I love the location. The walk to the office takes me right past Specialty's in the morning. Those muffins are murder on my girlish waistline."

They drifted toward Rayann's office while Teresa struggled with her unhappiness. Rayann had moved and she hadn't even known about that kind of significant upheaval. She didn't even know where she'd moved to.

What did she really know about Rayann? Did she go to Gay Pride? Did she like to dance? Who was her favorite artist? Did she like movies? Had she cried when Jadzia died?

She asked herself how she could possibly be in love. The very idea was ridiculous.

As she reached her cubicle she saw Diego putting something in her in-box. He tried to rev up around the corner when he saw her coming. "Negatory, my man. The three months were up two weeks ago."

Diego switched on his luminous eyes. "Just one last little ad?"

"No way. I'm through being your indentured servant. Go use those baby-seal eyes on someone else. I'm immune."

"You have a heart of stone."

Teresa picked up the art board and the revision worksheet as if it smelled. "I have enough of my own shitwork, thank you."

He gave her a wounded look that was all pretense and took the project back. "I wish I had some status around here."

"I wish I had a lifetime supply of C-cell batteries."

Diego hooted and buzzed away. He didn't know the half of it. She'd taken to hiding the ones she bought, even if it was an entire Costco economy pack. Vivian and Kim were not only still hot and heavy, they were addicts.

It was not fair that other people got to be in love.

Hoping to improve her spirits, she got out her mural design and studied the snapshots she'd taken of the soon-to-be garden lot and the surrounding buildings. When she'd visited the site she'd met with a few of the would-be painters — high school kids with not just enthusiasm, but some real talent as well. They'd sat down in the vacant lot amid the chunks of dirt and broken bottles and shown Teresa their own portfolios. It had felt strange, but not at all unwelcome, to have these kids all looking at her as the professional.

The garden would be a piece of nature in the center of concrete, asphalt and busy intersections. She'd decided on her concept: a mural that made the garden seem bigger, that let the flat lot seemingly fade into rolling hills covered with more flowers. It would be easy to paint by a group, too. If she measured out the line of sight properly, from the street it would look as if you'd found a door into the countryside. It would be visual space on a street that was one residential hotel after another.

"Is that for the garden project?"

For once she hadn't felt Rayann's approach. She

flushed. "Sorry, I know it's supposed to be on my own time."

"What own time? You're here so much there's no such thing. Can I see it?"

Teresa had printed some preliminary designs on cardstock so they could be leaned against each other for the three-dimensional effect. "Like this, so that the buildings all around are no longer buildings, but hills and sky."

"That's marvelous. And the yellow spectrum will reflect the weather conditions."

"I hope so. I don't want a blazing blue sky when it's raining. I want people to forget it's a mural." Rayann had changed her perfume. She smelled faintly of peaches. Great, Teresa thought. If I want to stay sane I have to give up peach Snapple.

"It's great. I can't imagine what would be better. This could really put you on the map as an artist."

Teresa found she could chuckle. "Instead of a lowly computer designer cranking out shampoo display ads?" She waved a hand at the stack on her desk.

"Maybe. You could move into freelance. But I'm not supposed to suggest that," Rayann said. "Jim will kill me. Philip will kill me. I will kill me."

"Well, it'll be a while before I have those kinds of options."

Henry slipped a file into Rayann's hands. "Philip is on his way down, too."

"Thanks, Henry." She glanced back at the mural designs. "It really is terrific work."

"Thanks." Teresa inhaled deeply when Rayann had left, catching the last of her scent before it drifted away. Her nose caught a whiff of something else —

something savory and mouthwatering. She stood up and peered over the top of the cubicle wall.

Philip was over near the elevators and behind him were white-clad caterers bearing steaming trays. Rayann was talking to him with a great deal of animation, then Henry threw open the doors to the big conference room. The caterers went in and a few moments later a blast of salsa music brought everyone to their feet.

Teresa lost no time at the buffet line. Lunch had been a long time ago. The reason for the celebration was passed word of mouth — a record earnings quarter. Folks from other departments began pouring out of the stairwell and elevators.

Sparkling cider had the same effect on Teresa as champagne. She found herself dancing while still holding her plate of Swedish meatballs and cheese. Gloria Estefan ordered her to do the Conga. She did.

She gorged herself on Calamata olives, then joined the dancing for the last of "La Bamba." The taped music switched to a really upbeat version of "In the Mood." Her feet loved swing music. Mike Freeman caught her by the hand and away they went. As she swung around she saw that Rayann was dancing with Jim Dettman. Swing was obviously not a big favorite for other people. Rayann and Jim were the only other couple.

The song was nearly over when Mike shouted, "Trade you," at Jim. Teresa collided with Rayann in the partner exchange and when the stars subsided realized that Jim and Mike had danced off with each other. The crowd was hooting with laughter.

Rayann's eyes were full of amusement. Teresa

shrugged and presented her hands, follower to leader. Rayann took them and swung her through a turn so quickly Teresa almost couldn't keep up. The crowd applauded and the song ended.

"Sorry." Rayann let go of Teresa's hands. "I haven't led in ages."

Teresa made room for an energetic group of hip-hoppers. "You were fine," she said. Rayann was flushed and smiling. She glowed with vitality. Looking at her hurt Teresa's eyes. She didn't know this Rayann, but she wanted to. She wanted to in the worst way.

"Time for more cider," Rayann said, and she walked toward the buffet without a backward glance.

The music was "Can't Touch This." A timely reminder, Teresa thought.

"Rayann, you are a sight for sore eyes!"

Rayann accepted Jill's bear hug. "I found myself with a free evening and my new digs are too empty to tolerate." Apart from a limited amount of bedroom furniture, a chair in the kitchen was the extent of the furnishings. The people who were buying the house in Oakland had run into a financing snag, so she had put off moving out any more of the furniture in case the house had to go back on the market.

"Where'd you move to?" Jill didn't seem in the least surprised that Rayann had moved. Then again, Rayann hadn't been by the bar since the memorial ten months ago.

"A condo south of Market. My mom knew the guy

selling it and I got a decent deal. My commute is now a fifteen-minute walk, which I can really use." She slid onto a barstool.

"What's your poison tonight?"

At one time she would have grimaced over Jill's choice of words. *Poison* was a little too close to home. But she knew she was back in control. "I'll take one of your Manhattans. It's been too long."

"An extra shot of bitters, right?"

"You have a marvelous memory, Jill."

Jill reached over the bar to tweak her cheek. "I always remember what my friends like."

It was a quiet night. No one seemed interested in dancing, so Jill had the jukebox on low. There was no sign of the back-up bartender, either.

"Danny will be here in a while," Rayann said. "I have to admit she's the one who called me. It feels like ages since we saw each other." The words were no sooner out of her mouth when the door banged open and Danny sauntered through.

Her hug was as enthusiastic as Jill's. "Corona, barkeep, and step on it."

Jill affectionately flipped Danny off, then brought Rayann's Manhattan and a chilled bottle of beer. No glass for Danny.

"You look great, Ray. How's life?" Danny asked.

Jill leaned on the bar and listened in.

"Life is good. Better than I thought it could be for a while."

"I'm glad for your sake." Danny chugged from the bottle. "Been a long day, but I made up my mind that I'm retiring. I have rebuilt my last engine. This guy at some technical school has been after me to teach Rolls and Mercedes engine repair and I think I'm going to do it. Hours are shorter, and it's decent enough pay considering I won't really be working and lots and lots of days off. Marilyn wants to buy a motorhome."

"It sounds ideal, Danny," Jill said. "You know what retired bartenders do?"

Danny shook her head.

"Tend bar."

"That's grim." Danny finished the beer and squinted into the empty bottle. "They're making these smaller."

"No, you're just drinking them faster."

"Well, hell. One's my limit."

"I'm going broke on customers like you." Jill went to the other end of the bar to clear glasses from a departing couple.

"Danny, I just wanted to tell you — thank you."

"For what?" Danny's inability to meet Rayann's gaze said she knew perfectly well for what.

"For all that you did while Lou was sick. I couldn't have made it through without you."

Danny tried to shrug it off. "There wasn't anything I wouldn't have done for Lou."

"And she knew that."

"I didn't realize she was dying until she was gone. I didn't want to accept it. I was sure the doctors were a bunch of fuckups."

"We all dealt with it in different ways."

"When my time comes I hope I can deal with it as well as Lou did."

Rayann raised her glass. "Hear, hear."

"To hell with my limit." Danny waved at Jill. "Barkeep, one more Corona, and step on it."

"And the horse you rode in on," Jill yelled back.

She delivered the Corona and uncapped a Diet Coke of her own.

"To Louisa," Danny said.

They clinked glasses.

Rayann didn't know what made her turn her head and look through the lattice into the café. But she was not surprised to see Teresa's eyes, gazing back at her.

Time only seemed to stand still, but it was a singular sensation. She felt at once pierced and made whole with the passion in Teresa's eyes. She remembered the fevered rush she had felt dancing with Teresa. It had only been a few moments and several weeks ago now, but she remembered it vividly with same fevered rush she'd felt then. It had been years and years since she had been the one to lead. It had felt good to flex that muscle and it reminded her of how heady it had been to know how much Teresa had needed her, wanted her.

Teresa seemed to be having a late dinner with a very good-looking woman — stylish to the max. A girl-friend, maybe?

It would be rude not to go and say something to her, Rayann thought. But Teresa wasn't getting up either. Had they come to this? Unable to manage the basic civilities because they couldn't keep their hands off each other? Rayann reminded herself she was in complete control. But she did not get up.

"You look like you just saw a ghost." Danny swiveled in the direction of Rayann's gaze.

"Just someone I work with."

"Speaking of ghosts, the weirdest thing happened a couple of nights ago. You know I don't believe in all that life-after-death crap, and I know damn well Louisa is having way too much fun wherever she is to be watching over the likes of me. But I was just about asleep when I had this compelling urge to turn on the TV to channel six. You know what was on?"

"What?"

"*All About Eve.* Lou's favorite movie."

Rayann spluttered into her drink. "I watched that, too. But I saw it in the TV guide."

"Well, it was weird. I was awake all night and I told Lou that I could do without that kind of experience."

"Do you think she heard you?" It took conscious effort not to glance in Teresa's direction, but she was dying to know if Teresa was still looking at her.

"Hell, I don't know. I felt better."

Rayann grinned. "You know, I talk to her sometimes, too. But I finally stopped getting answers."

Danny's smile was more wistful. "I know what you mean."

Danny shoved off a little bit later, and Rayann realized she had no reason to linger. She settled up with Jill and, without wanting to, looked at where Teresa had been sitting.

Teresa's dinner companion was heading out the door, leaving Teresa at the table with the last of her dinner.

She could not not say something to her. Avoiding Teresa was an admission that she was afraid of what would happen if they were alone together.

Teresa didn't look in the least bit surprised when Rayann stopped at the table. "Have a seat. I was just grabbing some dinner with my roommate, but I have to go back to the office."

"You work too hard." Rayann sat down. Roommate, not girlfriend. Oh stop, she told herself. It doesn't matter to you. "You work harder than I do, which by definition is too hard."

Teresa's smile was a little forced. "I'm just trying to impress the powers that be." The waitress dropped off her change and Teresa pocketed the coins and left the bills. "Well, I have to get back."

"I'm heading home — it's the same train."

They walked to the station together and leaned against the door rails even though there were seats available.

"What has you working late?"

"The color palette for Tichon. I know I shouldn't fuss so much when the printers will botch it anyway, but the presentation needs to be right."

"Too true. Did you ever see a movie called *Mr. Blandings Builds His Dream House*?"

Teresa shook her head.

"It's an old Cary Grant, Myrna Loy movie about building a house in Connecticut for the outrageous sum of fifteen thousand dollars. I always think of it when printers mess up the colors, because there's a great scene where Myrna Loy is giving samples to the painters. She goes from room to room. In this room robin's-egg, the next something between buttercup and sunshine. In the next it's a July leaf. She finishes explaining all of this to the painter and walks away. The painter goes over to the guy with the brush and says, 'Blue, yellow and green.' "

Teresa chuckled. "That's what it feels like sometimes. I feel as if I specify Pantone two-twenty-four and the printer just says, 'Something in the two hundreds.' "

Rayann did not find the silence that fell in the least bit comfortable. It made her fidget. When they pulled into the Montgomery Street station she got off, even though Embarcadero was closer to home. "I may as well pick up some reading material," she said.

Teresa just nodded. They were at the street level when Teresa stopped. "I . . . I don't feel like working tonight."

"There's no reason why you should."

They stood under a dim street lamp. Rayann found she could not make herself walk away.

"You wanted to know what I knew about pain. When you asked me that, I didn't have an answer." Teresa raised her chin. "I have one now. The answer is that everything I know about pain I learned from a master."

Rayann gasped. "How can you say that? I've tried —"

"It's nothing you've done. Or haven't done. It's just who you are. You still love her. You're still toasting her. You might be smiling more, laughing more, but she's always there. I think if I held you up to the light I'd see her face. It's just the way it is." A lone tear trickled across Teresa's cheek.

"It's the way it is now," Rayann managed. "I don't know about next week, or next year."

"You don't have to make me feel better." Teresa turned her face away. "If it's all I can have, at least let me have the pain."

"Teresa."

"Don't."

"Can we talk about it?"

"What's to discuss?"

What indeed. Rayann knew she should let it go. She cleared her tight throat and took what felt like one of the biggest risks of her life. "How about that I

233

can't forget the way you touched me? That I don't want to forget it?"

Teresa looked at her as if she was lying. She smiled bitterly. "Are you offering me more of the same?"

"Yes."

"Well, let's go then. Is your place far?"

This was not what Rayann had expected. "Not really, if you don't mind a walk."

"The sooner we start, the sooner we'll be in bed."

They walked in silence. Rayann dreaded arriving at her building. What did she really know about Teresa? What if this time they ended with recriminations instead of tenderness?

What was she doing?

Teresa tried to tell herself she was shivering because it was cold and not because she was both angry and frightened. She would not be a bed toy for Rayann while she got over the sainted Louisa. But she wanted to be in Rayann's arms again so badly that she was afraid she would accept those terms.

Would it really hurt for one night? Maybe it would flush Rayann out of her system. The harm was that one night could become two, she thought. Two could become four.

The building was perched on the bay shoreline, and Rayann's condo looked eastward toward Alameda and the glittering Oakland hills. Any other time she would have stopped to absorb the view, but instead Teresa unbuttoned her jacket. She spoke for the first time since they'd headed toward Rayann's. "Which way is the bedroom?"

Rayann winced. Teresa didn't know why she was trying to ruin things. Maybe she was hoping it would be really bad sex and she'd fall out of love.

Rayann gestured toward the hallway and Teresa made her way in the dim light to the only bedroom with any furnishings. They were spare — a double bed and a small dresser.

She went about taking her clothes off in a businesslike fashion.

"Teresa, why are you doing this?"

She stood there with her shirt off and in her bare feet. What was she supposed to say, that she was here because every cell in her body was crying out for Rayann's touch? The truth was too painful. She was here because she couldn't say no. She took the child's way out. "Because I hate you."

Rayann's gaze was devouring her breasts and her mouth had parted. When Teresa moved her hands to her zipper, Rayann's gaze followed.

Teresa's head whirled with the idea that she had any power over Rayann at all. She slowly pushed down her jeans, removing one leg at a time, then let them fall to the floor with a *whoosh*.

Rayann jumped at the sound. Teresa walked slowly toward her. When she was close enough to be touched, she stopped and waited. Rayann was breathing hard. Her eyes closed and then opened as if she couldn't help herself.

Touch me, Teresa willed.

Rayann's hands finally moved. She brought her fingertips to Teresa's hips. Gentle pressure made

Teresa step forward and she was enfolded in Rayann's arms.

Rayann held her, kissed her with bruising force. One hand was already pushing its way between Teresa's thighs. "This is what you wanted, right?"

Yes and no. She couldn't stop the tears she'd been holding in since she'd heard Rayann toasting her dead lover. "Yes," she managed through another harsh kiss.

She was on her back on the bed. Rayann was between her legs, her hand teasing. Teresa reached for Rayann's breasts and was confused when she found only clothing. Her body chilled. Rayann hadn't even taken her jacket off. This was not what she wanted. She didn't want to be just a body.

"No," she whimpered and she cursed herself for a weakling.

Rayann froze. After a ragged breath she stood up. Teresa was trembling with conflicting desires.

"Which is it?" Rayann's face was lost in the darkness.

Only the truth was left. She sat up. "I want this." Her voice broke. "I want you. I thought I could pretend it was just sex, but I can't."

Rayann dropped to her knees next to the bed. "I'm sorry. I was mean. I don't know why. I'm so afraid it *is* just sex and I don't want to use you."

"You still love her."

"Yes. Yes, I do." Rayann's voice was anguished. "I'll never stop. And I don't know yet if I can grow another heart." A sob turned into a laugh as she wiped her eyes. "I know that sounds corny."

"Yeah. Yeah, it does." Teresa had no idea what part of her found the ability to smile.

Rayann slid out of her jacket. "Let's start over."

Teresa unbuttoned Rayann's blouse as she ducked her head for a more tender kiss. It ended with their noses and cheeks brushing in a fevered exploration that led to fingers trailing over ears and under jaws, then lightly over shoulders.

Rayann joined her on the bed and Teresa held nothing back. She brought Rayann's hand to where she so badly needed her touch and buried her mouth in the heat of Rayann's breasts.

The answer was yes — the question did not matter. With each heartbeat Teresa found another well of desire only to have it quenched in the next flicker of Rayann's fingers.

She swam in Rayann after that. Gasping for breath, savoring the journey from thigh to shoulders. She found the pulse points that gave origin to the scent of peaches and the tender spots that made Rayann croon with yet more desire, then with satisfaction.

The answer was yes — the question did not matter.

13

"I thought this day would never end." Rayann rolled over in bed and turned on the light.

Teresa flinched from the sudden glare. "It was the longest day of my life. What the heck was everyone doing in your office all day?"

"No work talk," Rayann said. "It isn't important."

"You're right." Teresa coiled herself around a pillow. "I'm glad it's the weekend, though."

Rayann thought she looked delectable. The pang of guilt as she thought it was less today. But it was still there. She was glad they weren't sleeping in the big bed she'd shared with Louisa. She wasn't prepared for that yet. "What shall we talk about?"

"After what we just did, I feel brave enough to talk about us."

Rayann's heart fluttered with sudden panic. "Okay. You start."

Teresa sat up, all long lines and seductive nakedness. "I was wondering, well, getting up my nerve to ask."

"Ask what?" Rayann bit her lower lip.

"Would you like to go out to dinner with me? Maybe to a movie afterward?"

Rayann blinked. "You mean . . . like a date?"

"I believe that's what it's called. Not that we've ever done it. I think it would be good for us. We can't just leave work, walk here and have sex every night."

"Whyever not?" Teresa's eyebrows arched and Rayann blew her a kiss. "I'm just teasing. Okay, I can see how dating might be a good thing." Her lips twitched. "Can I expect good things on the first date?"

"How much are you going to spend on me?"

"How much do I have to spend?"

Teresa considered it. "Well, I'm not cheap. But I am on special this week."

Rayann giggled for what felt like the first time in a year. "What movie do you want to see?"

"There's a new Jackie Chan — or the new *Star Trek*."

Rayann wasn't quite sure what a Jackie Chan was. "There's a Kurosawa retrospective at the Embarcadero."

Teresa looked thoughtful. "Okay, we have some work to do there. For dinner?"

"Yeah?"

"Steak or seafood?"

Rayann tried to read Teresa's mind. "Seafood," she said finally.

Teresa heaved a sigh of relief. "Thank goodness."

They sat side by side against the headboard and shared the soda Rayann had found in the fridge.

"I'm going to ask a serious question," Rayann said. "I want the God's honest truth."

"Okay."

"Okay?"

"Absolutely."

"The dessert is chocolate. What do you like with it?"

"Like cake or ice cream?"

"Whatever, but it's chocolate."

"Well, caramel is okay. Or another type of chocolate. Cream, whipped or iced. But no fruit. I'm sorry, but that whole trend of ruining a great slab of chocolate with gritty, seed-filled something is grotesque."

Rayann sighed happily. "There's hope."

"But tell me this. Milk or dark?"

Rayann thought about it. "Yes."

Teresa laughed and finished the soda.

More softly, Rayann said, "I don't know where we're going. I can't promise if this is forever."

"I don't care if it is or isn't." Teresa hooked her pinkie finger with Rayann's. "All I want is for it to take a really long time for us to find out."

Rayann snuggled down in the bed. It was too small, but so far it had served its purpose. "This is wrong, you know. We're breaking several important policies."

"I know. If it becomes an issue maybe I'll go

freelance." Teresa's knee brushed against Rayann's thigh.

"But you love working at Liman's. I can tell."

"I like the people and I like most of the work. But I'm really excited about the mural and so very not excited about fussing over how much of a model's face the shampoo bottle should cover."

"I know what you mean."

"It would be like my fourth job in a year. I'm not champing at the bit to do it. But I will if I need to. A year ago I wouldn't have considered taking the risk, but now I could."

"Well, let's take it as it goes." Rayann trailed a lazy finger down Teresa's arm. "If you had a dream job, what would it be?"

"You mean other than being the one in charge of powdering Xena so her armor doesn't chafe?"

"I'm next in line for that one. You can powder Gabrielle."

"And work my way up to Xena? That does sound challenging . . . oh . . ."

Rayann liked the way Teresa inhaled sharply when something aroused her. She used just her fingernails on Teresa's breasts and was rewarded with a shudder. There was no guessing with Teresa, another way she would never confuse her with Louisa.

"I thought we were going on a date." Teresa arched her back.

"Who said anything about tonight?"

Teresa left Rayann in deep sleep. A trip to the bathroom was urgently required. She closed the door quietly and switched on the light. Her reflection startled her.

She approached the mirror slowly, ignoring her squinting in the light and the rumpled mess of her hair.

The wrinkle was having babies. And there were creases in the corners of her mouth. Love, pain, fear and hope — they showed. They were proof that she was alive. They were proof that she loved.

She decided right then and there that anti-wrinkle cream would never touch her face.

LOOKING FOR NAIAD?

Buy our books at
www.naiadpress.com

or call our toll-free number
1-800-533-1973

or by fax (24 hours a day)
1-850-539-9731

JUST YESTERDAY by Linda Hill. 176 pp. Reliving all the
passion of yesterday.   ISBN 1-56280-219-4   11.95

THE TOUCH OF YOUR HAND edited by Barbara Grier and
Christine Cassidy. 304 pp. Erotic love stories by Naiad Press
authors.   ISBN 1-56280-220-8   14.95

WINDROW GARDEN by Janet McClellan. 192 pp. They discover
a passion they never dreamed possible.   ISBN 1-56280-216-X   11.95

PAST DUE by Claire McNab. 224 pp. 10th Carol Ashton
mystery.   ISBN 1-56280-217-8   11.95

CHRISTABEL by Laura Adams. 224 pp. Two captive hearts and
the passion that will set them free.   ISBN 1-56280-214-3   11.95

PRIVATE PASSIONS by Laura DeHart Young. 192 pp. An
unforgettable new portrait of lesbian love . . .   ISBN 1-56280-215-1   11.95

BAD MOON RISING by Barbara Johnson. 208 pp. 2nd Colleen
Fitzgerald mystery.   ISBN 1-56280-211-9   11.95

RIVER QUAY by Janet McClellan. 208 pp. 3rd Tru North
mystery.   ISBN 1-56280-212-7   11.95

ENDLESS LOVE by Lisa Shapiro. 272 pp. To believe, once
again, that love can be forever.   ISBN 1-56280-213-5   11.95

FALLEN FROM GRACE by Pat Welch. 256 pp. 6th Helen Black
mystery.   ISBN 1-56280-209-7   11.95

THE NAKED EYE by Catherine Ennis. 208 pp. Her lover in the
camera's eye . . .   ISBN 1-56280-210-0   11.95

OVER THE LINE by Tracey Richardson. 176 pp. 2nd Stevie
Houston mystery.   ISBN 1-56280-202-X   11.95

JULIA'S SONG by Ann O'Leary. 208 pp. Strangely
disturbing . . . strangely exciting.   ISBN 1-56280-197-X   11.95

LOVE IN THE BALANCE by Marianne K. Martin. 256 pp.
Weighing the costs of love . . .   ISBN 1-56280-199-6   11.95

PIECE OF MY HEART by Julia Watts. 208 pp. All the
stuff that dreams are made of —   ISBN 1-56280-206-2   11.95

MAKING UP FOR LOST TIME by Karin Kallmaker. 240 pp.
Nobody does it better . . .   ISBN 1-56280-196-1   11.95

GOLD FEVER by Lyn Denison. 224 pp. By author of *Dream
Lover*.   ISBN 1-56280-201-1   11.95

WHEN THE DEAD SPEAK by Therese Szymanski. 224 pp. 2nd
Brett Higgins mystery.   ISBN 1-56280-198-8   11.95

FOURTH DOWN by Kate Calloway. 240 pp. 4th Cassidy James
mystery.   ISBN 1-56280-205-4   11.95

A MOMENT'S INDISCRETION by Peggy J. Herring. 176 pp.
There's a fine line between love and lust . . .   ISBN 1-56280-194-5   11.95

CITY LIGHTS/COUNTRY CANDLES by Penny Hayes. 208 pp.
About the women she has known . . .   ISBN 1-56280-195-3   11.95

POSSESSIONS by Kaye Davis. 240 pp. 2nd Maris Middleton
mystery.   ISBN 1-56280-192-9   11.95

A QUESTION OF LOVE by Saxon Bennett. 208 pp. Every
woman is granted one great love.   ISBN 1-56280-205-4   11.95

RHYTHM TIDE by Frankie J. Jones. 160 pp. . . . to desire
passionately and be passionately desired.   ISBN 1-56280-189-9   11.95

PENN VALLEY PHOENIX by Janet McClellan. 208 pp. 2nd
Tru North Mystery.   ISBN 1-56280-200-3   11.95

BY RESERVATION ONLY by Jackie Calhoun. 240 pp. A
chance for true happiness.   ISBN 1-56280-191-0   11.95

OLD BLACK MAGIC by Jaye Maiman. 272 pp. 9th Robin
Miller mystery.   ISBN 1-56280-175-9   11.95

LEGACY OF LOVE by Marianne K. Martin. 240 pp. Women
will do anything for her . . .   ISBN 1-56280-184-8   11.95

LETTING GO by Ann O'Leary. 160 pp. Laura, at 39, in love
with 23-year-old Kate.   ISBN 1-56280-183-X   11.95

LADY BE GOOD edited by Barbara Grier and Christine Cassidy.
288 pp. Erotic stories by Naiad Press authors. ISBN 1-56280-180-5   14.95

CHAIN LETTER by Claire McNab. 288 pp. 9th Carol Ashton
mystery.   ISBN 1-56280-181-3   11.95

NIGHT VISION by Laura Adams. 256 pp. Erotic fantasy romance
by "famous" author.   ISBN 1-56280-182-1   11.95

SEA TO SHINING SEA by Lisa Shapiro. 256 pp. Unable to resist
the raging passion . . .   ISBN 1-56280-177-5   11.95

THIRD DEGREE by Kate Calloway. 224 pp. 3rd Cassidy James
mystery.   ISBN 1-56280-185-6   11.95

WHEN THE DANCING STOPS by Therese Szymanski. 272 pp.
1st Brett Higgins mystery.   ISBN 1-56280-186-4   11.95

PHASES OF THE MOON by Julia Watts. 192 pp. . . . . hungry
for everything life has to offer.   ISBN 1-56280-176-7   11.95

BABY IT'S COLD by Jaye Maiman. 256 pp. 5th Robin Miller
mystery.   ISBN 1-56280-156-2   10.95

CLASS REUNION by Linda Hill. 176 pp. The girl from her
past . . .   ISBN 1-56280-178-3   11.95

DREAM LOVER by Lyn Denison. 224 pp. A soft, sensuous,
romantic fantasy.   ISBN 1-56280-173-1   11.95

FORTY LOVE by Diana Simmonds. 288 pp. Joyous, heart-
warming romance.   ISBN 1-56280-171-6   11.95

IN THE MOOD by Robbi Sommers. 160 pp. The queen of
erotic tension!   ISBN 1-56280-172-4   11.95

SWIMMING CAT COVE by Lauren Douglas. 192 pp. 2nd
Allison O'Neil Mystery.   ISBN 1-56280-168-6   11.95

THE LOVING LESBIAN by Claire McNab and Sharon Gedan.
240 pp. Explore the experiences that make lesbian love unique.
                                   ISBN 1-56280-169-4   14.95

COURTED by Celia Cohen. 160 pp. Sparkling romantic
encounter.   ISBN 1-56280-166-X   11.95

SEASONS OF THE HEART by Jackie Calhoun. 240 pp. Romance
through the years.   ISBN 1-56280-167-8   11.95

K. C. BOMBER by Janet McClellan. 208 pp. 1st Tru North
mystery.   ISBN 1-56280-157-0   11.95

LAST RITES by Tracey Richardson. 192 pp. 1st Stevie Houston
mystery.   ISBN 1-56280-164-3   11.95

EMBRACE IN MOTION by Karin Kallmaker. 256 pp. A whirlwind
love affair.   ISBN 1-56280-165-1   11.95

HOT CHECK by Peggy J. Herring. 192 pp. Will workaholic Alice
fall for guitarist Ricky?   ISBN 1-56280-163-5   11.95

OLD TIES by Saxon Bennett. 176 pp. Can Cleo surrender to a
passionate new love?   ISBN 1-56280-159-7   11.95

LOVE ON THE LINE by Laura DeHart Young. 176 pp. Will Stef
win Kay's heart?   ISBN 1-56280-162-7   11.95

DEVIL'S LEG CROSSING by Kaye Davis. 192 pp. 1st Maris
Middleton mystery.   ISBN 1-56280-158-9   11.95

COSTA BRAVA by Marta Balletbo Coll. 144 pp. Read the book,
see the movie!   ISBN 1-56280-153-8   11.95

MEETING MAGDALENE & OTHER STORIES by
Marilyn Freeman. 144 pp. Read the book, see the movie!
                                   ISBN 1-56280-170-8   11.95

SECOND FIDDLE by Kate 208 pp. 2nd P.I. Cassidy James
mystery.   ISBN 1-56280-169-6   11.95

LAUREL by Isabel Miller. 128 pp. By the author of the beloved
Patience and Sarah.   ISBN 1-56280-146-5   10.95

LOVE OR MONEY by Jackie Calhoun. 240 pp. The romance of
real life.   ISBN 1-56280-147-3   10.95

SMOKE AND MIRRORS by Pat Welch. 224 pp. 5th Helen Black
Mystery.   ISBN 1-56280-143-0   10.95

DANCING IN THE DARK edited by Barbara Grier & Christine
Cassidy. 272 pp. Erotic love stories by Naiad Press authors.
                                   ISBN 1-56280-144-9   14.95

TIME AND TIME AGAIN by Catherine Ennis. 176 pp. Passionate
love affair.   ISBN 1-56280-145-7   10.95

Diane Salvatore. 256 pp. Erotic and wickedly
ıle about the business of learning to live
                              ISBN 1-56280-114-7   10.95

Ilaire McNab. 208 pp. 8th Carol Ashton
                              ISBN 1-56280-135-X   11.95

ORAL HISTORY by Susan Johnson.
nore?   ISBN 1-56280-142-2   14.95

arin Kallmaker. 240 pp. By the undisputed
nance.   ISBN 1-56280-139-2   11.95

THE GIRL NEXT DOOR by Mindy Kaplan. 208 pp. Just what
you d expect.   ISBN 1-56280-140-6   11.95

NOW AND THEN by Penny Hayes. 240 pp. Romance on the
westward journey.   ISBN 1-56280-121-X   11.95

HEART ON FIRE by Diana Simmonds. 176 pp. The romantic and
erotic rival of *Curious Wine.*   ISBN 1-56280-152-X   11.95

DEATH AT LAVENDER BAY by Lauren Wright Douglas. 208 pp.
1st Allison O'Neil Mystery.   ISBN 1-56280-085-X   11.95

YES I SAID YES I WILL by Judith McDaniel. 272 pp. Hot
romance by famous author.   ISBN 1-56280-138-4   11.95

FORBIDDEN FIRES by Margaret C. Anderson. Edited by Mathilda
Hills. 176 pp. Famous author's "unpublished" Lesbian romance.
                              ISBN 1-56280-123-6   21.95

SIDE TRACKS by Teresa Stores. 160 pp. Gender-bending
Lesbians on the road.   ISBN 1-56280-122-8   10.95

WILDWOOD FLOWERS by Julia Watts. 208 pp. Hilarious and
heart-warming tale of true love.   ISBN 1-56280-127-9   10.95

NEVER SAY NEVER by Linda Hill. 224 pp. Rule #1: Never get
involved with . . .   ISBN 1-56280-126-0   11.95

THE WISH LIST by Saxon Bennett. 192 pp. Romance through
the years.   ISBN 1-56280-125-2   10.95

OUT OF THE NIGHT by Kris Bruyer. 192 pp. Spine-tingling
thriller.   ISBN 1-56280-120-1   10.95

LOVE'S HARVEST by Peggy J. Herring. 176 pp. by the author of
Once More With Feeling.   ISBN 1-56280-117-1   10.95

FAMILY SECRETS by Laura DeHart Young. 208 pp. Enthralling
romance and suspense.   ISBN 1-56280-119-8   10.95

These are just a few of the many Naiad Press titles — we are the oldest and
largest lesbian/feminist publishing company in the world. We also offer an
enormous selection of lesbian video products. Please request a complete
catalog. We offer personal service; we encourage and welcome direct mail
orders from individuals who have limited access to bookstores carrying our
publications.